I0597486

Ge-Mi Part One

A hundred years ago, evil scientists spliced human genes with those of animals, creating a genetic mutation passed on through the generations. Hated because of their differences, these Ge-Mis live on the fringes of society where they scrounge and scrape to get by.

Nevada is half Ge-Mi and hides that fact behind baggy clothes and by keeping distance between himself and everyone around him. One day, his peaceful life is shattered by an explosion and the arrival of a pack of wolves to sniff out the culprit.

Wolves have excellent noses and as Alpha, Taylor can sniff out every one of Nevada's secrets—and the harder Nevada tries to resist, the more difficult staying away from Taylor becomes.

Ge-Mi Part Two

Taylor Reyes was born to privilege, but despite that has always been considered an abomination. He was the child that should never have been born and has spent his life trying to prove his worth to the world to no avail. As a red wolf Ge-Mi, humans look at his furry ears before his accomplishments, and no matter how hard he continues to work Taylor knows that will never change. Still, he has a grandfather that loves him and a pack of his own to lead. The life he created for himself is not a bad one, until one day a pair of adorable cat ears derails everything.

The thought of finding a mate had never crossed Taylor's mind, but suddenly he can't stop thinking about Nevada. There's no time for the distraction, though, as people are moving to unseat his grandfather from the city's throne. The fight has just begun, but ending it might mean Taylor will lose Nevada forever.

Ge-Mi Duology

Mell Eight

A NineStar Press Publication

www.ninestarpress.com

Ge-Mi Duology

© 2021 Mell Eight

Cover Art © 2021 Natasha Snow

This is a work of fiction. Names, characters, places, and incidents are either the product of the author's imagination or are used fictitiously. Any resemblance to actual persons living or dead, business establishments, events, or locales is entirely coincidental.

All rights reserved. No part of this publication may be reproduced in any material form, whether by printing, photocopying, scanning or otherwise without the written permission of the publisher. To request permission and all other inquiries, contact NineStar Press at the physical or web addresses above or at Contact@ninestarpress.com.

Printed in the USA

ISBN: 978-1-64890-232-1

First Edition, March, 2021

WARNING:

This book contains depictions of graphic violence.

Ge-Mi

Part One

Prologue

In the waiting room, people milled about restlessly. There weren't any chairs provided for the supplicants, nor for the onlookers who were only there to enjoy the show. Handing over a bribe wasn't supposed to be a comfortable experience, after all.

Nevada stood in a corner, the backpack, containing the only thing he had that would suit as a bribe, clutched carefully in his arms. Rosto stood next to Nevada, one shoulder pressed indolently against the wall. He was older than Nevada by at least twenty years, his hair grayed at the temples, but his back still strong and unbent. Rosto had done this before—brought a supplicant with his bribe—and he had a personal connection with the lord of the city. Rosto wasn't worried, but Nevada was.

It had only been six months since Mom had died. They hadn't had the money or the resources to get her proper health care, and her cold had turned deadly far too quickly for Nevada's three part-time jobs to pay for a doctor's bill. It wasn't just that the doctor was expensive, but payoff money for his silence was too much. Nevada would have risked it for Mom's sake, but Mom had put her shaking and weak foot down and the matter was settled.

After that, Nevada hadn't been able to stay in that house or city. The hiding was a fact of life, but he hoped the melancholy could be alleviated with a new home and a new start. Nevada had arrived in Kensey three days ago and found an apartment whose owner didn't mind pets. The down payment had sapped the last of his hastily scraped-together funds, so Nevada had gone job hunting.

Rosto's café was quaint and in need of a full-time waiter. The pay was decent and the hours reasonable. But in Kensey, things worked differently than Nevada's old home. The lord in Kensey wanted a direct bribe from every citizen; the previous lord didn't pay any mind to peons like Nevada. Had Nevada known he had to meet with the lord directly and provide a bribe that, if accepted, was his ticket to having any sort of life in Kensey, he might have chosen to settle in a different city with a different lord.

The room fell silent quickly, almost suddenly, as a side door opened. The man who stepped into the room first was clearly a guard. He was wearing a light layer of armor, the bluish metal vibrant against his dark skin, and a large laser gun at his hip. His hard eyes surveyed the room once before he stepped aside. The second man who walked into the room looked like he was Rosto's age, somewhere in his late fifties. His blond hair disguised whatever gray may have been present, but the crow's feet around his blue eyes revealed his true age.

"Where is Taylor?" the lord asked his guard. They both walked to the front of the room where a very large desk built of thick, dark wood was positioned. It was intimidating, but that was probably the point.

"Off with his wolves," the guard replied stiffly.

"That boy," the lord grumbled. "All right, let's get started."

A third man stepped forward from where he had been standing off to the side of the desk. He was holding a datapad from which he read out the first name.

A woman and her two young children approached the foot of the desk. She needed help finding her layabout husband. He owed her back wages for childcare, and she wanted him to pay up. Her bribe was a gold necklace with a ruby in the center, which would have paid for the childcare handsomely.

"She's after revenge," Rosto explained under his breath. "Her husband was a cheat, and she wants what's rightfully owed to her because she knows he'll suffer for it. Lord Reyes prefers supplicants ask for something meaningful, instead of straight out asking for something purely selfish. He's a good man."

Nevada hoped so because he didn't have anything nearly as nice as a ruby necklace in his bag.

For the next half hour, he watched as fancy watches, jewelry, and other expensive items were offered to Lord Reyes in return for favors. Some of them Lord Reyes agreed to, like the woman looking for childcare money, but others he denied. He didn't return the bribes either way.

"Rosto Gregorio," the steward called.

"That's us," Rosto grunted as he pushed off the wall. He strode forward, unconcerned, and Nevada hurried to follow.

They reached the desk and stopped a few feet away. Rosto bowed, and Nevada copied him a beat too late.

"How's the café?" Lord Reyes asked, a smile on his face. It was the first smile Nevada had seen from him. He apparently was interested in what Rosto had to say.

"We're expanding the kitchen at the moment," Rosto immediately began to explain. "Putting in four ovens so we can sell fresh-baked goods as well. We're also adding outside tables for the summer, which means I need additional waitstaff. I'm looking to hire Nevada here."

Lord Reyes turned his attention to Nevada, and Nevada fought not to squirm. He needed the job, which meant Lord Reyes had to like him.

"New to the area, too, I believe," Lord Reyes said. "Has all the appropriate paperwork been filed?"

"As of last night," Rosto replied. "All it needs is your seal of approval."

Lord Reyes nodded. "You'll have to come over for dinner and tell me about your renovations," he said to Rosto. His attention switched back to Nevada. "What have you brought to entice me to allow you to live and work in my city?"

Nevada gulped and reached into his bag. He knew what he looked like. He had a ragged bandana tied tightly over his head, his long-sleeve shirt was threadbare and unraveling at the cuffs, and his loose jeans had a darned hole in one knee. The clothes were baggy, too, but Nevada had to hide a pair of cat ears and a tail beneath his outfit. He looked poor, but hopefully that meant Lord Reyes wouldn't look any deeper at what Nevada was hiding. Hopefully, it also meant he wasn't expecting anything extravagant as Nevada's bribe.

Nevada pulled the fluffiest, whitest cat he had ever fostered out of the bag and gently placed her on the desk.

"This is Princess Pea. She likes big houses and lots of attention. She's also very particular about what blankets she sleeps on. I thought you might like to have her company."

The waiting room had gone silent. It was even quieter than when Lord Reyes had first walked into the room. Yes, it wasn't a ruby necklace, but surely a beautiful cat wasn't so bad. Nevada fought to keep from turning to look around the room.

Lord Reyes's eyes had frozen in a hard glare. "Is this a joke?" he snapped.

Nevada bit his lip, wondering how to answer that. Maybe live animals weren't acceptable as a bribe? Before he could formulate an answer, Princess Pea took over. She sauntered across the desk toward Lord Reyes and hopped down into his lap where she promptly began to purr furiously. One of Lord Reyes's hands involuntarily drifted to his lap where he began to pet her soft fur.

"Fine," Lord Reyes snapped. "Six months' probation. Rosto will come report to me then, and I'll decide whether to accept you in my city. I'll even make sure Princess here isn't eaten," he added cryptically.

Rosto bowed, one of his hands pushing on Nevada's shoulder to force Nevada to bow also. Then that hand pushed Nevada toward the door.

"I can't believe you got away with that!" Rosto breathed once they were out of the waiting room and headed toward the building exit.

"Got away with what?" Nevada asked, glad to be away from Lord Reyes.

Rosto laughed, but he didn't sound amused. "You gave Lord Reyes a cat. That's practically the ultimate insult."

"Oh," Nevada mumbled, feeling his shoulders droop. He had six months, at least, which was enough time to save up before he had to move to another new city.

"Where did you find that cat anyway?" Rosto asked as they reached the main doors and headed out into the parking lot.

"I find cats everywhere," Nevada replied with a shrug. "I have a beautiful tortoiseshell looking for a new home, if you're interested."

Rosto unlocked the car without answering. Nevada got in and buckled his seat belt. The engine whirred to life, and the hydraulics bounced them gently into the air. The car flew toward the city down the hill, Rosto guiding them along in silence. They stopped a few minutes later outside Nevada's apartment building.

"No more cats where Lord Reyes is concerned, okay?" Rosto said. The car idled in the air for a few seconds as the hydraulics engaged and the car drifted to the ground. "You start on Monday, 9:00 a.m. sharp."

Nevada got out of the car and stepped onto the curb. Rosto waved goodbye before sending the car streaking upward again.

Chapter One

"So, whaddaya think?" a man asked the person sitting across from him as Nevada carefully set two large cups of black coffee onto the table. The man was fat and had sweat stains down the back of his T-shirt. The second man, on the other hand, wore a three-piece suit and tie and looked totally unimpressed with his companion. "There's a niche market for what I'm selling. All I need is some money to get me off the ground."

Nevada added a cup of creamer and a dish holding individually packaged sugars to the table and then returned to his tray to grab the plate with the three extra-large chocolate muffins the larger man had ordered.

"You won't make it," the second man was saying as Nevada returned. "Not in this city or any other. You don't have the required connections."

"Connections," the fat man scoffed. "All I need is to buy a storefront, and the money will start coming in. I'll have you paid back within the first year."

"Take this coffee shop, for example," the other man continued evenly. "The owner had to get the proper permits to build or renovate when he bought the property, and then he also had to get permits for food and drink, and to pass the health inspections. Who do you think owns the permit department that allowed this café to remain open? And how do you think, with your pathetic connections, you would be able to do the same? In this city, and in any other town or city, you have to know someone or be someone to get something. You lack either of those redeeming qualities."

Nevada gathered up his tray and left his customers to their chat. He had other tables to mind, and it wasn't as if it was any of his business what kind of struggle the fat man was dealing with to earn enough to get by. Nevada had his own paycheck to watch.

Another table had been filled in his section a few minutes ago. Enough time had passed for them to look at their menu, so Nevada headed over. "Welcome to Café Spice," Nevada said with a wide smile at the elderly couple. They were passing a pair of reading glasses back and forth as they read through the menu. "My name is Nevada, and I'll be your server for the afternoon. Is there anything I can help you with?"

"The print is too small," the man warbled. "Tell your manager to fix that!"

"I'll have a scone," the woman replied, serenely ignoring her husband's grumbles. "And two herbal teas, honey, no sugar."

"Will that be all?" Nevada asked, mostly to the woman because her husband was still muttering to himself under his breath and squinting at the menu.

"Yes, dear. Thank you."

Nevada collected the menus after a long moment while the wife tugged ineffectually at the menu her husband was holding. He had to grump a few more times before he gave up.

"I want a scone too," the man argued as Nevada headed to the back counter to input their orders into the computer.

"Not with your diabetes. I'll let you have a bite of mine."

The computer pinged softly when the order was received, and Nevada turned to go check on his other tables.

Then there was an explosion.

The floor shook, and Nevada's ears rang with the awesome thump. Plaster floated down from the ceiling, and the front window had a spiderweb crack running through it, but it appeared some other storefront had been the target.

Pieces of broken cups were scattered on the floor, interspersed between overturned tables. The old man was on the floor, hovering protectively over his wife and yelling about laser cannons and shock shields. Nevada wouldn't be surprised to learn the man had fought in the last Great War, when all the large cities had been demolished and the current status quo of smaller cities and towns owned and controlled by single lords had begun.

The man in the suit looked totally unconcerned, standing tall while everyone else was still cringing. He had his phone pressed to his ear, and as an eerie cackle filled the street outside the coffeehouse, he was the one who said, "Hyenas."

"Damned Ge-Mis," a woman snarled across the room.

The cackle grew and was echoed by other laughing hyena howls. The loudest was female, as it should be when it came to matriarchal hyena packs.

Nevada remained with his back pressed against the counter. His tail had bottle-brushed in fright, and he needed a few secret moments to calm himself again. It helped that he wasn't the only one with raised hackles in the shop. In a small basket next to the computer, Nevada's latest rescue project was hissing and spitting; the infant kitten's own tiny tail was twice the size of his head. Nevada reached into the basket and pulled Hex to his chest.

The motion was soothing both to him and the kitten. Rosto had given the kitten the name Hex when Nevada had first brought him in. The kitten was all black, but he had a white stripe down his spine that stuck up like spikes whenever Hex was upset. When Nevada had found him, Hex hadn't yet managed to open his eyes, but he had gotten separated from his mother and needed help, which Nevada was happy to provide.

Nevada's tail finally smoothed out. He kept happy thoughts of rescuing kittens in his head while he tucked his tail back between his legs and wrapped it around one leg where it wouldn't be noticeable through his baggy pants.

The last echoing cackle finally faded from the street outside, and startled patrons were slowly getting back to their feet. Nevada tucked Hex into the breast pocket of his black uniform shirt and hurried to find a broom. He needed to get the smashed porcelain off the floor before someone cut themselves. The closet where the cleaning supplies were kept was off the kitchen, and Nevada had just stepped inside when the first howl flitted through the air. The hyenas had struck, but the wolves were on the hunt to catch and stop them. Nevada gripped the broom tightly and took a deep breath. The shiver of fear had to work its way down his spine and through his tail. The tip twitched irritably where it was curled around Nevada's knee, but otherwise he was able to force his fear to subside.

He hated dogs. They were mean and liked to bite and chase for no good reason. Well, they could chase those nasty hyenas, so long as they stayed away from Nevada.

Rosto was busy bustling around the customers. He was helping them back into their chairs while Nevada's coworker, Leslie, was pouring free cups of coffee or tea to soothe frayed nerves. It didn't look like anyone had been hurt in the shop, so Nevada hurried to get the broken cups and spilled food and drinks cleaned before someone slipped. Rosto gave Nevada a smile of approval when he saw what Nevada was doing.

No one wanted to leave the café just yet. The hyenas were gone, allegedly, but there was safety in numbers, and comfort too. Plus, the wolves might be working for the city, but they were still Ge-Mis on the prowl and from a human mindset should be avoided.

Things were finally settling down in the shop when the front door popped open again.

"Smells like cats in here," a gravelly voice barked. Three wolves stepped into the café, and any vestiges of relief in the air immediately vanished. The wolves weren't bothering to tone down what they were. The one who had spoken looked wild. His wolf-gray hair was uncut and flyaway, but his pointed ears still managed to show on the top of his head. There was an eagerness to his eyes and his step as he looked across the room that spoke of running and hunting and killing his prey.

The second wolf behind him was female. Her brown-and-black hair was also long and wild, her pointed ears poking through her hair, but her wildness was contained behind yellow eyes that saw everything as she scanned the café. Her nose was a darker color than the rest of her skin. On a human it would have been an unfortunate birthmark, but it was the most blatant show of her heritage Nevada could see on either of the wolves.

The first two wolves stalked forward, heading directly toward the man in a suit.

"Carley, we think we've found their den, but the damned things have scattered," the male wolf said with a snort and a huff of air through his nose. "Seriously, it reeks of cat in here."

"If they're scattered, they can't plan and execute another attack," Carley replied as he brushed a bit of plaster dust off his suit's starched collar. He didn't appear to notice the way the wolf was scratching at his stomach through his loose T-shirt with a set of long, pointed nails. "Drew, you've done well. Why don't you and LeeAnne continue the search? If you can catch at least one hyena, we may be able to learn their final plans."

"You got it!" Drew replied. His long, fluffy gray tail was wagging furiously behind him, making some of the customers cringe away. LeeAnne's tail wagged also as they both turned and bounded out the door. They ducked their heads to the third wolf, still lounging against the doorjamb, before heading out into the street.

"Drew is right, you know," the third wolf said softly. Nevada felt a shiver go down his spine and through his tail again. The voice was gentle and soothing, very un-wolf-like, yet there was still the slightest touch of menace to the tilt of his head and the flash of his very blue eyes. His hair was human-colored, light blond, and cut fashionably to frame his face, but where his wolf ears poked through, the hair turned red. His tail, from where Nevada could see it poking through the back of his jeans, was also red.

"Drew is right about what, Taylor?" Carley sighed. He was busy digging out his wallet from his back pocket. He dropped a few dollars onto the table to pay for his coffee, right in front of where the fat man was still hyperventilating, and then began walking to the door.

"It does reek of cat in here."

"Well, congratulations," Carley sighed. "You have a good nose. But right now, we're trying to catch the hyenas. You can investigate the cat smell later. You know what your grandfather would say."

Taylor let out a long breath of air through his nose and then shook himself like a dog from ears to tail. "Yeah, yeah. Gramps wants the job done first and playing saved for later. Let's go, then."

The door shut behind them, leaving a silent café in their wake. Slowly the second shock wore off, and patrons began to gather their families and their belongings to head out the door. After today's excitement, Nevada had doubts there would be many more customers coming in.

"That was Taylor Reyes," the fat man burbled. "Taylor Reyes!" Nevada knew most of the other patrons lived in the city and knew who Taylor was. The fat man was the only stranger, and it was clear he wouldn't be staying in the city for long.

Nevada had never met Taylor Reyes before. He knew the Reyes family, of course, although since his first introduction, he hadn't met Lord Reyes again. Three years had passed and, looking back, Nevada couldn't believe he had survived bringing a cat to Lord Reyes. He had learned the rumors since then and knew how bad of a faux pas he had committed.

No one knew whether Lord Reyes's teenaged daughter had been raped or if she had chosen to sleep with a Ge-Mi. The rumor mill supplied a new version of the story every few years, but the end of the story was always the same: she had died in childbirth, leaving behind a newborn red wolf Ge-Mi. Instead of tossing the babe out, or sending it to a special orphanage, Reyes had done the unimaginable. He had kept the child and raised Taylor as his heir. Over time, Taylor had shown his gumption as a true son of the Reyes family. He was Alpha of a local pack of wolves who, sometimes overeagerly, policed the city on behalf of the family. Taylor also ran much of the Reyes business interests, to the consternation of the employees he had to interact with. The latest rumor going around the city was that Grandpa Reyes was ill, and Taylor was going to have to fight with his cousins to keep his place when Grandpa died.

But all that was beside the point. Nevada had a café to clean and damages to assess.

It took the rest of the afternoon to get all the ceiling plaster and spilled drinks off the tile floor. The plaster had dissolved when it got wet and had stuck to the tile. Hex had gone back into his basket after a quick bottle of warmed lunch while Nevada spent the hours on his hands and knees trying to scrape up the goopy bits. Leslie had started a damage report to submit to Lord Reyes, including the cracked ceiling, windows, dishes, and tables. Rosto had begun the heavy task of carting the broken furniture and many trash bags out to the dumpster.

It was well after dark by the time Nevada and Hex could leave. It was only a little later than the end of his shift, but he felt doubly as exhausted as usual. His apartment was a few blocks away, an easy walk when

Nevada wasn't so tired. He trudged along the darkened sidewalk with his head down. He had a bag full of leftovers from the café in his hand, so he didn't need to worry about dinner, but if he didn't get a shower in before he keeled over in bed, he would feel nasty in the morning.

The shop the hyenas had targeted was a total loss, Nevada saw as he walked past the blasted storefront. The fire was out and the fire crew long gone. It still smelled faintly sour, like the oxygen suppressant that had been used to put out the bomb-induced blaze, but the smell of burnt plastic and wood prevailed. It had been a stationary shop, but Nevada had never seen any customers inside when he had walked past. He could smell blood in the air, too, so someone had died. But then, the shop owner was one of the more vocal humans who liked to talk about castrating Ge-Mis so they died off. After hearing that in conversation one too many times, Nevada had refused to buy any paper supplies from that store, but there were other reasons that had caused humans to also dislike the shop owner. He hadn't been a nice man.

Nevada kept walking. Home was so close, which meant time to sleep was nearing. He had walked completely past the opening of the alley across the street from the blast before Hex stiffened in his shirt pocket. Nevada heard the cry a moment later and quickly backtracked.

The alley was dark—the streetlamps didn't reach far—but Nevada's eyesight in the dark was very good. It didn't take long to locate his quarry. The tomcat had probably been napping when the explosion occurred and hadn't been able to move quickly enough to get out of the alley before some heavy boxes fell on him. He had scratched and crawled until his body was free, but his tail was still stuck.

"Oh, you poor thing," Nevada gasped. Hex added his own soft meows from Nevada's pocket. The tomcat yowled, but didn't hiss or bite when Nevada carefully reached forward to shift the heavy box off the cat's tail. The cat jumped away, staring suspiciously at Nevada, but after a few moments he crept forward and began to tentatively sniff Nevada's bent knee. "I have food," Nevada explained, "and soft beds. At least until your tail gets better."

The tomcat meowed stiffly and allowed Nevada to gently pick him up. Nevada ran a gentle hand through the cat's fur, searching for broken bones, but found only bruises. He let out a sigh of relief and walked out of the alley feeling a little better about his day. It was always a good day when he could help a cat in need.

They walked the last few blocks in silence until they reached Nevada's apartment building. Nevada pressed his thumb to the scanner on the door. It beeped softly and turned green as the door clicked unlocked. The elevator waited to take him to the top floor.

Nevada hadn't needed to look twice before putting down money on his apartment. It was perfect for his needs, and the landlord didn't mind pets. The landlord had once lived in the entire top floor with his family, but once his daughter was looking to move out on her own, he had renovated. The result was a large apartment for the landlord and his wife, an empty-nest couple, and a private apartment next door for their daughter. When the daughter had gotten married, she had moved out, and Nevada had been lucky enough to answer the ad first.

He unlocked the door with his key. The security was a little lacking—there weren't any proper retinal scanners or DNA checks—but with the wolves patrolling the streets to keep crime down, Nevada didn't mind that the electronic lock was broken. The landlord had promised to fix it soon.

A chorus of meows greeted him as Nevada stepped inside. He only had six cats living with him at the moment, Hex included, but sometimes it seemed like there were more. Beth sauntered across the hardwood floor, her tail waving like a flag. She was an ordinary-looking brown queen, but she was so unbelievably friendly that, had she wanted to leave, he could have found her a happy home. Instead she was content to be the mother cat, bossing everyone around and taking complete charge of his apartment.

She yowled imperiously up at Nevada.

Nevada smiled when Hex roared back, his baby voice trying so very hard to emulate Beth. Nevada passed Hex down to Beth, who immediately grabbed him in her mouth so he wouldn't run off before his bath.

"I also brought home a new tom," Nevada said as he gently placed the adult cat on the ground next to Beth. "Show him around, teach him the rules."

Beth snorted and meowed pointedly at the tom before stalking off toward her corner with Hex in unhappy tow. Nevada dropped his bag of food onto the counter and headed to the bathroom.

The apartment was all one room, with the kitchen on one side and the living area on the other. There was an open storage loft high along the opposite wall with the sleeping area and bathroom below. Nevada had converted the sleeping space into a cat home with scratching posts, climbing structures, and hanging feathers to bat.

He closed the door to the bathroom behind him to keep any curious cats out and started to strip. His pants came off first, his tail happy for the respite. It was long and extremely fluffy, pure white in color except for black rosettes down the length. He pulled his shirt off next. His chest was purely human, thin and lightly muscled, but his back was not. A line of white fur ran from the nape of his neck down to his tail. Across his back, black rosette birthmarks were spread across his skin like ornate tattoos.

On his head was an oversized handkerchief that he had carefully folded into a triangle and tied down tightly. His hair was the white of unblemished snow, except for the streaks of black that, when cut short, revealed even more black rosettes, but that wasn't the reason he kept his head so carefully covered. Two gently rounded cat ears sat on top of his head. They were small and easily hidden— his mother had called them cute—but they and his tail were the only two parts of him that would definitively pinpoint him as a Ge-Mi.

Nevada turned on the hot water in the shower with a grimace. The shower was necessary after a long day working at the café. He couldn't give himself a tongue bath—his spine wasn't nearly flexible enough for that—so it was the human way of getting clean or nothing. Not for the first time, Nevada wished his father had been a tiger or some other water-loving cat. Instead Nevada was half snow leopard.

A quick shampoo of his hair and tail and a layer of soap later and Nevada was done. He hurried out of the water and into a towel, glad it was over. The cats were all hidden away when Nevada emerged from the bathroom. He grabbed the bag of food from the kitchen, walked out into the middle of his apartment, and turned toward the storage loft. He bounced on the balls of his feet twice before leaping into the air and then allowed himself to fall into the loft. Nevada landed on the soft pillows and quilts that comprised his bed with a thump.

He pulled on a pair of soft boxers backward so he could pull his tail through the hole, and then snuggled deep into his covers to eat his leftover muffins. He drifted happily off to sleep a few minutes later, purring softly to himself.

Chapter Two

Beth had all the cats neatly organized in front of their food bowls the next morning, including the new tom, who looked suitably chastised. Nevada had woken to the sounds of Beth yowling and hissing at him to get him in line. By the time Nevada had climbed out from under his covers and jumped down from the loft, the matter had been settled. Food was more important than fighting anyway. Nevada could feel his back burning as six pairs of cat eyes tracked his progress through the kitchen to the cabinet that held their food. He filled six bowls and brought them over to the waiting cats as quickly as he could.

Hex, the only cat too young for solid food, had found his own breakfast. A few months ago, Nevada had found Maya stumbling through a busy pedestrian street, faint with hunger and heavy with pregnancy. Three days later she had given birth to four healthy kittens. Those kittens had just been weaned when Nevada brought Hex home. Finding homes for the kittens hadn't been an issue, and Maya had consented to take care of Hex for a few extra weeks.

With all the cats happy, Nevada returned to the kitchen to find his own breakfast. He quickly scrambled some eggs and toasted a bagel. He spread a light layer of cream cheese on his warm bagel and then topped it off with thick slices of lox before digging in. He couldn't help letting out a few purrs of satisfaction at the taste of the smoked salmon, echoing those of the cats licking their bowls clean on the floor.

Nevada savored the last bite of lox for as long as he could before cleaning the kitchen and going to find a new uniform shirt to wear. He got dressed, tied his scarf tightly over his ears, gently gathered a sleeping Hex, and headed out the door to work.

A demolition crew was examining the burned store as Nevada walked past. A glass truck was pulled up in front of the café, and workers were removing the cracked front window as Nevada edged around them to get inside. Rosto was standing in the middle of the café, hands on his hips and an exasperated scowl on his face.

"You couldn't have told me any of this last night?" he asked, and Nevada saw the suited man named Carley from the previous afternoon standing next to a giant hole in the wall that certainly hadn't been there when Nevada had left the night before. The shop next door, where the hole led, had been empty for a few days. The owner had moved, but rumor said he hadn't paid his bribes on time. Nevada thought the man had retired and left to live nearer to his family.

"Lord Reyes decided last night that it was high time you expanded your café again," Carley explained with a shrug that was anything but apologetic. "The chef who will be organizing the restaurant portion should arrive any minute, and we can begin going over blueprints."

Nevada edged past them both as he headed toward the back of the shop where Hex's basket was located. He tucked Hex into the blanket and then leaned against the counter until Rosto finished arguing with Carley.

"Nevada," Rosto sighed when Carley walked off to meet with a man Nevada didn't recognize who had just come from the store next door. "As soon as the glass guys take off, roll some tables and chairs outside. We can set up an outdoor café until the indoor repairs are done."

The pastry chef had apparently been hard at work that morning despite the disaster cleanup going on around them because the front counter was fully stocked with all of their baked goods.

"You'll be our waiter outside for the morning rush, and Leslie can handle the cappuccino machine and the to-go orders inside."

Nevada nodded and headed toward the stack of tables they had deemed salvageable the day before. They could fit four of the round ones comfortably outside normally, but since they weren't going to have any seating inside, Nevada decided to tuck a few of the square ones out of the way too.

The day crawled. By the time an unblemished new front window had been installed in both the café and the empty shop next door, the time for the morning rush had passed. One or two people had braved the construction to get their coffee fix, but the majority of their customers had found somewhere else to go for the day. The tables outside indicated they were open and serving, but the usual lunch crowd never surfaced. The half-dozen customers they did have all looked scared and shifty as the blatant reminder of the explosion only the day before was attacked by a wrecking crew. It took the entire afternoon to level the burnt shell of the building across the street.

The only high point in Nevada's day was Hex's meowing and spitting in his basket. Every time the ground thumped from one of the heavy construction tractors touching down so the engineer guiding it could reassess the demolition, Hex's basket shook and upset him. Nevada kept Hex's stomach full, and since there were long stretches where there weren't any customers, he kept Hex entertained with a length of string on the floor.

The second day was much like the first. They had a larger morning crowd as their customers realized they were actually open despite the repairs that still needed to be done. The lunch crowd was larger, too, but they never had anyone waiting for a table. Customers drank their coffee and ate their muffins before hurrying back to work.

The wolf pack was much more active in the café's neighborhood that day, howling excitedly as they pursued the trail of the hyenas, which only added to the customers' anxiety. The café might have had more patrons had their inside seating been available, where the illusion of safety provided by four walls might have alleviated some of the worry.

After the lunch rush that never came, the chef and three men in hard hats arrived in the shop next-door. Rosto joined them, and the sounds of arguing punctuated the after-work crowd. Nevada went home that night with a headache and a distinct wish for all the issues to be resolved already. He wanted the café to return to normal so his easy, everyday life could continue unhindered.

On the third day after the explosion, things did start to settle down. Nevada walked to the café like usual. Hex sat in the breast pocket of Nevada's work shirt, two paws and his head sticking out the top so he could see everything and meow fiercely at it. The destroyed shop was completely gone. All of the rubble from the demolition had been removed sometime in the night, but it didn't look like any new construction had begun.

The café had a new sign hanging over the window. The original café still declared itself to be Café Spice, but the sign over the additional shop next-door read "Restaurant Spice." It wasn't very imaginative, but it worked.

Rosto was outside, dragging the tables and chairs back inside. Nevada waved to him as he walked past. He settled Hex in his basket and found his work apron before heading back outside to help. The inside of the café looked as if it had never been damaged. The ceiling was newly plastered and the walls repainted. The giant hole in the wall between the café and the restaurant had been evened and smoothed into an arch. A second, smaller arch had appeared overnight in the kitchen area, and the pastry chef, Marion, was still yanking baked goods out of the ovens. She was grumbling to herself, too, which Nevada understood because she was usually finished and off work by the time Nevada arrived. The construction crew must have interfered with her baking.

Hex reluctantly curled up in his basket. He apparently wanted to see more interesting things, not take a nap. Nevada tied his apron around his waist and hurried back outside to help Rosto.

"I'm sure you've noticed that Lord Reyes has decided to expand the café," Rosto said from across the table Nevada was helping him muscle through the door. Nevada didn't answer, too busy trying to keep his fingers from getting crushed by the doorframe, but Rosto didn't appear to want a response. "We've been sent an Italian chef, and I've permission to hire another part-time employee. Nevada, I'd like you to work in the restaurant, if that's okay. I want the new employee to get used to the café environment first."

"That's fine," Nevada answered with a shrug. He didn't really care so long as he had a job.

They pushed the table into place and hurried back outside to grab another one. "Do you have any suggestions or requests for the restaurant menu?"

Nevada didn't have to think. "Fish," he answered. If there were leftover pastries or muffins at the end of the day, Nevada got to take them home as a free dinner. If there was lots of fish left over, he could have a real treat.

Rosto let out a snort of laughter, and they had to put the table they were carrying down so he could catch his breath. "Sometimes I wonder if you're not part cat, the way you act like little Hex every once in a while." He walked over to the basket where Hex was meowing for attention. His tiny front paws and the tips of his ears kept appearing over the lip of the basket as he jumped around.

Nevada ducked his head so Rosto couldn't see his expression. The first time Rosto had said that to Nevada was two weeks after he had first started working at the café. Nevada had been on his hands and knees in the back alley, trying to convince a stray to come out of the trash compactor before she got hurt. Nevada had jumped and blubbered excuses at the time. Years later, Nevada still had to hide the flash of apprehension that always flitted across his face.

Sometimes Nevada wondered if Rosto had guessed what Nevada really was. He knew about all the stray cats Nevada took in. He even supported Nevada by allowing Hex and other motherless baby kittens to stay in the café during the day so Nevada could take care of them. Did Rosto suspect that Nevada was a Ge-Mi too? Nevada didn't know, but he worried about it.

Ge-Mis were genetic mutants: humans whose genes had been spliced with those of animals about a hundred and fifty years ago. The scientists of the time had been seeking a way to enhance human hearing and vision in order to prevent diseases like macular degeneration and hearing loss, but there were other scientists interested in the program too: scientists whose morals were less than ideal.

They wanted the advanced speed, the built-in weapons of claws and teeth, the agility, and the fierce survival nature of the animals. They wanted to create a super human—a creature with all the thinking and reasoning abilities of a human coupled with the advanced traits of animals. What they had then wanted to do with said creatures had never been released to the public, and after the war fifty years ago, most of the information had been lost in its entirety anyway. When the police forces of the time had raided the lab, they had found thousands of different human-animal species locked away in cages.

As intelligent humans, the creatures couldn't be cruelly confined in zoos or new, more humane, research labs. Instead, the government had ensured they had gotten an education so they could become normal, functioning members of society. None of which changed the fact that when a bear Ge-Mi got riled up he could knock down walls or a snake Ge-Mi could accidentally bite and poison someone when he felt threatened.

Even Nevada, who kept his sharp nails filed human-short, could out jump and outrun every other human around him. When Ge-Mis realized they could outrun the police and commit crimes normal humans couldn't, the stigma against them began to grow. Entire criminal gangs of Ge-Mis eventually formed. They were a minority at first, as most Ge-Mis were more than happy to work a regular nine-to-five job and raise their kids in their cookie-cutter houses, but as employers started to discriminate their hiring based on race, those law-abiding Ge-Mis had to turn to other means of survival as well, and the current status quo had evolved.

It wasn't illegal to be a Ge-Mi in the postwar world, but should a Ge-Mi walk into Rosto's shop, Rosto could refuse to provide service, and no one would fault Rosto for it. Rosto could fire Nevada on the spot for being half snow leopard, and the customers who smiled at him and chatted happily with him almost every day could light the torches and get out their pitchforks to ensure Nevada never returned.

The only exception to that social rule Nevada had ever seen was Taylor Reyes, but that was because his last name carried more weight than his tail and ears. Stupid dog.

They got the tables set up and brought in the chairs in time for the morning rush. The fright of the past few days had faded and the gossip had begun. Hyenas in wolf territory, in Reyes territory? Something was obviously up, but whether it was hyenas being stupid or something more sinister had yet to be determined.

One of Nevada's regulars got a bit riled up, insisting it was an evil plan hatched by the Ge-Mis to take over the world. "They're starting with their advance troops, you see," the man insisted, one hand fisted in Nevada's sleeve as he slurred drunkenly. "Send in the crazies like the hyenas to shake us up and then start sending the snakes to assassinate important people. Next thing you know, Reyes will be replaced with a lion claiming to be king of the jungle. You wait and see."

He finished his spiel and let Nevada go before pulling a silver flask out of his pocket and doctoring the fresh coffee Nevada had just brought him. There were people who had been listening, some rather intently, but at the sight of the flask, many of them rolled their eyes and returned to their own drinks. After all, the rumblings of a drunken man couldn't be true. But still, the idea was planted and everyone shifted in their seats for a few more minutes.

Nevada did his best to stay out of the conversation. Hyenas blowing things up was bad, but not all Ge-Mis were violent. He knew that firsthand.

As one week became two and no further violence occurred, fears died down entirely. Nevada didn't have time to worry about any of that anyway, because he spent all of his time studying the new menu and wine list. Selling a few muffins and a couple of different styles of coffee was easy in comparison to a full-course Italian menu with wines and specials. A few days before the restaurant was set to open, they had a tasting with all the employees gathered around one table, stuffing themselves on linguini and manicotti. Nevada tasted everything, and it was all delicious, but the stuffed sole was the best. Once everyone had a taste, Nevada pulled the plate a little closer and finished off the rest of the fish. It was soft and buttery, poached in milk and gentle spices that enhanced the simple nature of the fish. He was practically purring when he finished.

He had never before tasted anything so good. In his life, fish came in cans or sealed plastic. Either it was the lower-grade stuff made into cat food or the higher-level fish canned for human consumption. Nevada had eaten both in his life. The lox he ate was frozen in its plastic packaging before he bought it. Mama hadn't been able to afford fresh fish often, and if the taste of the sole was any indication, she hadn't really known how to cook it properly when they could get some.

"I think it's official," Rosto laughed. "If there's ever any fish left over, it goes home with Nevada."

Nevada opened his eyes and swallowed his last bite. Everyone was staring at him, but they were all smiling. Apparently, his getting blissed out over a piece of fish was funny. He double-checked that his tail hadn't started waving lazily in the air behind him in happiness as he felt his cheeks get hot.

"I've never tasted something so good before," Nevada tried to explain.

"I can add a fish cake to the appetizer list," the new chef murmured to himself. "And have a second selection as a weekly special."

Rosto nodded. "I like that idea."

Nevada's blush increased. They didn't have to change the menu just because he loved to eat fish. The manicotti was damned good, too, and those were only pasta and cheese. Nevada also wouldn't mind having a second taste of that chicken dish. That had been yummy too. In fact, the only thing he hadn't liked was the dish with too many onions. He had a human digestive system, so things like onions, grapes, and chocolate wouldn't make him sick or kill him, but he still didn't like them all that much.

"We'll have a soft opening in two days," Rosto continued, "and the grand opening in two weeks. Thanks for all your input as we take this step forward. With all your help, we can make this a success, and make Lord Reyes proud of his investment." Which was as much a warning as a speech of appreciation. Mess this up and you'll have to explain why to Lord Reyes.

Everyone nodded seriously at Rosto's words, Nevada included. Nevada didn't want any more scrutiny to land on him either. It was bad enough being known as the idiot stupid enough to bring Lord Reyes a cat as a bribe. The restaurant failing would make it so much worse.

Two days later, the restaurant opened. Nevada and Leslie had split the small restaurant down the middle, each taking the tables on either side of the door. Nevada worked the morning rush at the café like normal and then moved over to the restaurant side when it opened for lunch. The soft opening had been well advertised, and Nevada knew they had a full reservations list for the evening. Lunch was their trial run to hopefully work out the kinks in the system before that night.

It went smoothly enough. Rosto had ensured Nevada and Leslie both knew how the restaurant worked: where to get drinks, how to submit the food orders to the kitchen, and how to properly wait on tables. He was also there to greet everyone and give a hand whenever it was needed.

Nevada took an hour off for his own lunch around three o'clock. He had a muffin and some tea heavy with milk while also feeding Hex an afternoon snack. Rosto had given Hex lunch, but the kitten was growing a little more every day and was guzzling down multiple bottles as a result. Hex fell asleep in Nevada's lap when he was done eating, so Nevada put him back in his basket before returning to work.

Sing, the part-timer Rosto had hired just that week, gratefully relinquished Nevada's tables and returned to the café. Rosto would make sure Sing received the tips from his hour working, including the tables already in progress that Nevada was taking over.

There was a lull until five thirty, and then suddenly the restaurant was full, the tables bursting with people and food and the café filled with patrons waiting for a table to open up. Nevada had never felt so run ragged in his life as he hurried from table to table. His feet hurt from running around so much, his arms hurt from carrying heavy trays of food, and his head hurt from all the noise. Even his tail hurt where it was curled around his knee. He kept bumping it into chairs as he squeezed between the tables. If it continued to be this busy night after night, Rosto was going to have to hire a third waiter for the shift and split the restaurant into thirds.

Around seven thirty, the busboy cleared one of the smaller tables on Leslie's side of the room, and Rosto didn't seat anyone there despite the long line. Nevada was too busy to do more than curiously note the anomaly, but he did notice when the room suddenly fell silent.

Taylor Reyes stalked through the front door of the restaurant. He was scowling, and his tail was pressed firmly against his butt instead of waving happily in the air. He was not a happy wolf, which sent a shiver down Nevada's spine.

"Your table is ready," Rosto said genially, immediately hurrying forward to guide Taylor. "Will the rest of your party be joining you?"

The table was set for three, Nevada noted, but he had food to pick up in the kitchen so he turned to leave the room.

"Gramps decided to stay home, but Carley should be here in a minute," Nevada heard Taylor growl unhappily before Nevada walked into the kitchen.

The new chef was having the time of his life. His first restaurant's opening was going amazingly well, and his food was receiving compliments. Nevada loaded his tray, but before he could lift it onto his shoulder, Sing pushed through the curtain covering the arch between the café's kitchen and the restaurant's. He was carrying Hex's basket.

Hex was mewling piteously at the top of his lungs. His cries turned insistent when he saw Nevada.

"You can't come into the restaurant with me!" Nevada grumbled. Hex mewed in disagreement.

"He can't stay in the café," Sing said. "Some of the customers are complaining."

Nevada sighed. He reached out and plucked Hex from his basket and held the tiny kitten up so Nevada could stare Hex in the eyes.

"You have to behave in the restaurant," Nevada insisted, adding a touch of authoritative growl to his voice. Sing hurried back to the café with Hex's basket. Hex meowed in agreement that he would behave, so Nevada tucked him into his breast pocket and returned to his cooling tray of food.

Rosto had bribed all the appropriate people so a health inspector wouldn't make a stink about Nevada carting around a live animal near the food. Hex had also learned how to behave in the café during the weeks he had been coming with Nevada to work, so Nevada wasn't worried.

Nevada took his tray out to the waiting table and served them, then took orders from two more tables. He hurried to the back of the room where the drink station was set up to get both tables started. Leslie cornered him there.

"He keeps growling every time I get near the table," she grumbled. "I haven't even gotten their drink order yet!"

She could only mean the table where Taylor was sitting. Nevada peeked around the edge of the partition wall and saw that Taylor was slumped angrily in his seat across from the man in a nice suit Nevada remembered from the bombing. Carley was speaking, and it looked like Taylor was occasionally grunting to show he was actually listening.

Nevada didn't want to go anywhere near that table. He hated dogs. They made his tail quiver, and they barked and yelled and chased. Plus, Taylor had a good nose.

Nevada remembered his insistence that the café smelled like cats after the hyena bombing. Rosto had easily brushed it off thanks to Hex and the other cats Nevada had brought by over the years, but Nevada didn't know what might happen should Taylor get a close-up sniff of Nevada. Still, Leslie wouldn't have asked for Nevada to take the table if she thought she could handle it. Her hands were tucked into her apron, but Nevada thought he could see them shaking slightly. Leslie was scared of the Ge-Mi, just like everyone else.

What would she say if she knew that Nevada was one of them too?

Nevada sighed and nodded. "I'll take the table if you take the big one in the corner." Nevada pointed at a table that had just filled with a family with four rowdy kids. Leslie grimaced, but apparently it was the lesser of the two evils because she nodded. Nevada delivered drinks to the two waiting tables and then hurried over to Taylor's table.

He stood closer to Carley than Taylor, hoping that would help keep Taylor away. Nevada felt slightly shivery inside, and the tip of his tail was batting lightly against his knee. He fought to keep it still before someone noticed the odd movement.

"Welcome to Restaurant Spice," Nevada intoned. "May I take your drink order?" He smiled at them, hoping he didn't look too forced. Taylor didn't look in Nevada's direction, but Carley returned Nevada's smile.

"I'll have a glass of the house pinot grigio. He'll have water," Carley said genially. He didn't seem to notice that Nevada had neglected to introduce himself.

Taylor let out a snort of air. "I am old enough to have alcohol!" he snarled.

"You're not acting like it," Carley replied with apparent unconcern for Taylor's mood. Some of the other patrons at nearby tables were subtly trying to move their chairs farther away. Another shiver traveled down Nevada's spine and through his tail, but he forced his knees to stand firm. Taylor wasn't mad at him, and the last thing Nevada wanted was to run away in fear and call on Taylor's instincts to chase and catch.

"Vodka rocks," Taylor insisted, turning to glare at Nevada for the first time. His nostrils flared as he breathed heavily.

"Just water," Carley disagreed. He still hadn't lost his smile, and he was studying the menu as if he was more concerned about what he was going to order to eat than Taylor's temper.

Taylor jumped to his feet with a growl. "I wanted to have dinner with my pack, not be dragged to this place and dictated what I can order!" he snarled as he stalked around Carley's chair. Carley didn't turn to face Taylor even when Taylor stood at his side panting heavily. "Plus, this place still smells like cats! I hate it!"

He continued breathing heavily like a dog trying to cool down after a long run. Every other breath held a growl in it. Nevada froze in place when Taylor jumped up because the alternative was to jump himself, and he didn't really want to get outed as a Ge-Mi because they had to peel him off the ceiling.

"I hate cats, and I hate being dragged places I don't want to go!" Taylor continued to rant.

"I'll have the chicken piccata," Carley added to Nevada. "Taylor, what would you like to eat?"

Taylor snarled and turned on Nevada. "Why does this place reek of cats?" he hissed. "Why do you smell so much like a cat?" He sniffed at Nevada, bending closer until his nose was practically in Nevada's collar. Nevada shivered in place, unable to move. Taylor was going to reveal his secret and attack him all at once. Nevada braced himself for Taylor's teeth as he stepped closer to get a better sniff.

But then, Taylor jumped back with a howl. Little Hex had darted out of Nevada's pocket and clamped his baby teeth around Taylor's nose. Hex's claws scratched at Taylor's cheeks as he fought for purchase, and Taylor whined and yelled in pain.

"Get it off!" he screeched, and Nevada darted forward to rescue Hex before Taylor could hurt him.

Taylor caught Hex by the white scruff of the kitten's neck and yanked Hex off his face. He held Hex out at arm's length while Hex continued to spit and snarl and scratch at Taylor's wrist. Taylor's face was bleeding, and he snarled at Hex, which didn't deter Hex in the least. Nevada reached out and gently pried Hex from Taylor's grip before Hex could bite him again.

Rosto jumped between Nevada and Taylor, and Nevada quickly backed away. He held out a towel so Taylor could mop his face while pushing Nevada toward the kitchen with his other hand.

Nevada went, cradling a still-spitting Hex in both hands. He couldn't help glancing back over his shoulder before the kitchen door swung shut behind him. Carley was laughing hysterically at the table, Rosto looked worried, and one very blue eye glared at Nevada from behind the towel. Another shiver went down Nevada's spine and worked its way through his tail as the door finally closed.

"Bad Hex!" Nevada said. He knew he was supposed to scold the little kitten for attacking someone, but Nevada couldn't help but be relieved that Hex had been there. One more sniff and Taylor would have either uncovered Nevada's secret, or Nevada would have outed himself when he scurried away in fear. Hex's intervention, though violent, couldn't have been better timed. Nevada cradled Hex close in thanks as his own shivering finally slowed.

"Order up!"

Nevada turned to look, saw the food was for one of his own tables, and steeled himself. He had to get back to work, and the table was far away from Taylor. Nevada tucked Hex back into his pocket, where Hex immediately wriggled around until he could stand on his hind legs and poke his head and front paws out of the opening, and went to wash his hands. Nevada filled a tray with the dishes before tentatively poking his nose out the kitchen door.

Taylor was gone, Nevada saw with relief. Carley sat alone at his table sipping idly at a large glass of white wine. Rosto caught Nevada's eye as Nevada moved to the table waiting for their food and pointed at himself and then Carley. Nevada didn't need to worry about that table anymore; Rosto would handle it.

Nothing happened for the next hour. Taylor didn't return, and the patrons and Nevada gradually relaxed. Nevada's tail finally stopped twitching as the monotony of taking orders and delivering food returned. He was up near the front of the restaurant taking a drink order from a table when Carley finished eating and stood to leave. He left a few folded bills on the table and walked purposefully toward Nevada.

Nevada couldn't scurry away to hide in the kitchen. He had to wait while a little girl decided if she wanted soda or lemonade, and Carley was waiting at Nevada's shoulder when Nevada could finally leave.

"You're the idiot who offered Lord Reyes Princess Pea," Carley stated baldly. He reached out and gently rubbed Hex between the ears where he was still sitting in Nevada's pocket. Hex purred and batted playfully at Carley. "Still collecting cats, I see. You know, despite the fact Lord Reyes does like Pea, he was still going to toss you out of his city for the insult. Then Rosto came over for dinner one night and explained that you had about five cats living with you and had coaxed a sixth to safety in front of his eyes. Lord Reyes understands that you were young and too stupid to do any research about his city before offering your bribe. He will laugh hysterically when he hears about this little guy going after Taylor."

Nevada knew he shouldn't, but he had to offer anyway. "I have a tomcat that would love to have a house of his own where he's not being bossed around by the queen at my apartment," he said leadingly. "If you're interested."

Carley laughed. "I'll have to ask my wife." He smiled for a few more moments before shaking his head on some sort of internal thought. "Be careful around Taylor. Getting his nose bitten won't deter him for long."

With that one last worrying comment, Carley nodded in goodbye and swept out of the restaurant. Nevada hurried to get drinks for the table he had just left and to go to the kitchen to collect more food for another table.

The hours passed slowly, but by ten o'clock the place had finally emptied out. Nevada sank gratefully into a vacated chair. Leslie and Rosto joined him a few moments later.

"We need another busboy," Rosto murmured as he looked around the restaurant with fierce satisfaction on his face. Lord Reyes may have forced the upgrade on him, but Rosto was going to own it and make it thrive, and he was going to do it proudly.

"And another waiter," Leslie insisted. "Half the restaurant is too many tables for me."

The chef wandered out of the kitchen with four large plates precariously perched on his arms. Rosto took them and set one in front of each chair. The chef sat in the final seat around the table and watched with satisfaction when Nevada dug eagerly into his plate of salmon in a light dill sauce.

Rosto sent everyone home once they had finished eating. Hex had been snoozing in Nevada's pocket for hours—he hadn't even woken to beg for some dinner—but Rosto still shot the tiny paw sticking out a sidelong look.

"Maybe don't bring him along tomorrow," Rosto said with a sad shake of his head. Hex would be upset, but with Maya to take care of him, Nevada didn't need to worry about leaving him behind. Nevada nodded and stepped out of the restaurant into the cool evening.

He was beyond exhausted, but the tips in his pocket were far too nice a prize for him to feel bad about it. Nevada was supposed to work the morning shift in the café, but Rosto had pushed his starting time to eleven. The new part-time help could handle the morning if Nevada and Leslie had to stay late every night.

It was considerably later than Nevada usually walked the dark sidewalks back to his apartment. The city was a safe one—no one really wanted to catch the attention of Taylor's pack of wolf Ge-Mis by doing something violent—but he couldn't help walking a little faster than usual. He almost felt as if there were eyes on his back, tracking his every movement. Nevada hoped it was his imagination hyped up from the long and exhausting day combined with the scary confrontation with Taylor. Nevada just needed to shower, hug a few cats, and crawl into bed.

He felt a little better when the front door of his apartment building was locked behind him. Nevada hurried up the stairs and locked himself into the confines of his own apartment before he finally let out a quick breath of relief.

A chorus of meows greeted him. Nevada said hello softly and then carefully transferred the still-snoozing Hex from his pocket into the nest of blankets the other cats had created for Hex.

"I'm going to shower and then head to bed," he told Beth when she yowled at him. She rumbled unhappily, upset he didn't have the energy to see to her every need at the moment, and stalked away from him with her tail high in the air and disgust in every step.

Nevada followed exactly what he had told her. He showered quickly to get the day's sweat and smells from the restaurant out of his fur and then hopped up into his loft to pull on his usual pair of boxers that left his tail free. He was almost asleep amid his soft blankets and pillows when Beth yowled a warning. Half a second later, his front door popped open, and Taylor Reyes strode inside with a dark scowl on his face.

Chapter Three

"I didn't even need to track you from the restaurant," Taylor sneered. "I should have just followed the stench of cat. I could smell your apartment from blocks away."

He hadn't looked up yet to find Nevada. His eyes were tracking across the room below Nevada's perch. After one pass didn't reveal Nevada, Taylor growled.

"Come out, cat lover," he hissed. "You insulted me today, and I will get even no matter how well you think you're hiding."

Nevada's tail had bottle-brushed the second the door had popped open. He didn't dare move to reveal himself with his tail and ears out in the open. Nevada had a feeling Taylor would love to destroy the home Nevada had made here by exposing him.

Taylor also didn't know that he was surrounded. A low, rumbling growl escaped from Beth as she stalked out into the open. The tomcat leaped up onto the kitchen counter behind Taylor with a yowl of his own. Maya jumped down from the cat tree she had been lazing on and circled so she was on Taylor's right side. Omni, another of his rescue projects, flanked Taylor's left side. Eventually, all of Nevada's adult cats were hissing and snarling at Taylor as they surrounded him. The noise woke Hex, who added his own voice to the melee and crawled out of his nest to join Beth in harassing Taylor from the front. His white crest was flared aggressively, which only made him more adorable.

"You think your cats will stop me?" Taylor growled with a sniff of disdain. "I owe the little one a bit of pain after he attacked me today. Maybe I'll share it with the rest of your cats too!" He flexed his claws purposefully, still looking around the small apartment for Nevada. He hadn't looked up yet; instead, he focused on the bathroom door Nevada had left slightly ajar. Still, Nevada shivered at the threat in Taylor's voice. He had no doubt Taylor would make good on his threats.

"Don't hurt them," Nevada begged.

Taylor looked up immediately at Nevada's words. His wild grin stilled as shock replaced his fury when he caught sight of Nevada.

"You're one of us?" He gaped upward, staring at Nevada's rounded ears and oversized tail. Nevada nodded and brushed his white-and-black hair out of his eyes.

Taylor opened and closed his mouth a few times, as if he couldn't decide what he wanted to say, and then he spun on his heel and stalked back out the door without saying anything. The tomcat let Taylor go with one last warning hiss, and Taylor slammed the door behind himself.

Nevada waited a few long seconds to see if Taylor would return. When it became clear Taylor was gone, at least for the moment, Nevada jumped down from his perch and hurried to lock the door again. He had no idea how Taylor had unlocked it in the first place, which was pretty damned worrying.

He had a bag of cat treats in a drawer the cats couldn't get to easily. Nevada passed them out to everyone including Hex, who was getting too big to stay on a diet of formula for much longer. He would be weaned and ready for adoption very soon, which was another distressing thought to add to Nevada's list for just that night. His cats came and went. Some he found homes for; others decided it was time to head back into the wild. Beth had decided her home was with him simply because she felt he needed a queen to help manage his household, but all the others— Hex included—would probably be gone within the year. Hex was the first kitten Nevada had really gotten attached to. Something about his fierce personality, like he was a lion instead of a baby kitten, made Nevada want to keep him.

Nevada knew he couldn't, though. Hex would want a home and an owner to lord over without Beth or Nevada to force him in line.

A yawn stretched Nevada's face as the adrenaline from Taylor's abrupt visit faded away and the exhaustion from his long day returned. There would be repercussions for everything that had happened that day; he had no doubt of that. Taylor still hadn't gotten his revenge for Hex attacking him, and now that he knew Nevada's secret,

Nevada had little doubt Taylor would take advantage of it in some way.

Nevada would pack a bag in the morning just in case he had to run. He was too tired to worry about it now. Every time he tried to think of possible scenarios, his eyes drifted shut. Nevada put the cat treats safely away, gave everyone a quick rub down their back and Hex a belly rub that had the kitten purring happily, and then jumped back into his loft. He drifted to sleep biting his lip and hoping the morning wouldn't be any worse.

*

The only difference Nevada noticed the next morning when he walked into the café was the fact that he had to leave Hex at home. Hex had cried and complained, but Rosto didn't want him for a few days, and Nevada had to obey his boss. Instead of having him work in the café for the first hour before the restaurant opened, Rosto sent Nevada to make sure everything was properly set up in the restaurant. Nevada ensured all the tables were set; then he began working through the reservation list and marking down which tables were taken at what times. It took the entire hour before he was finished.

Leslie unlocked the restaurant door and flipped the sign to open at exactly noon. They waited for any lunchtime customers to arrive. Nevada knew it would take time for the locals to change their routines to make Restaurant Spice their lunch destination of choice. Many people still just wanted their coffee and muffin from the café instead of a full, sit-down meal, so there was only a slow trickle of people for the first few hours.

Leslie had two tables of customers, and Nevada was about to hand over his lone table to Sing at three o'clock when the door opened and Taylor stepped inside. He walked up to the waiter's stand where Rosto hurried over from the café side to greet him.

"I'll take the chicken parm sub to go," Taylor told Rosto as Nevada started inching his way back toward the kitchen where he would be out of sight. "Excuse me."

Taylor hurried around Rosto and through the restaurant directly toward where Nevada was trying to sneak off. Nevada didn't have a chance to run before Taylor was in front of him.

A hooked finger pulled the breast pocket of Nevada's uniform open as Taylor checked briefly for hidden attack kittens while simultaneously muscling Nevada backward until he was pressed against the nearest wall. Taylor's nose pressed into the side of Nevada's neck, and Nevada heard him breathe in deeply.

"You really do reek like a cat," Taylor said softly, a low growl in his voice. Nevada suppressed another shiver, but couldn't stop the tip of his tail from twitching in agitation against his knee. He wanted the dog off now before Taylor bit and snarled and got really unpleasant, yet Nevada didn't dare move and accidentally incite Taylor. "But without the house cats covering for you, I can tell what you are. It's a smart camouflage."

Taylor smelled like musky dog, but he also smelled like soap. It was a clean scent Nevada couldn't help sniffing appreciatively. It was strange having a body pressed so aggressively against his—and scary—yet Taylor was so warm, and the heat that penetrated through Nevada was soothing. He could almost forget it was a damned awful dog menacing him, rather than a more welcome companion.

Nevada firmly told his brain to shut it. He needed to stay focused on reality, not on some strange fantasy. Taylor could bite him at any moment, and being pressed against the wall like this meant Nevada had very little chance of defending himself.

Still, the tufts of red hair around Taylor's pointed ears were directly under Nevada's eyes, and Nevada's traitorous brain couldn't help noticing how beautiful the brilliant shade of red emerging from his otherwise very blond hair was. Taylor's nose moved lower to sniff along Nevada's collarbone, and now Nevada could see the rest of the restaurant.

Leslie was standing between her two tables, Sing was hovering awkwardly in the archway between the café and the restaurant, and everyone else in the room was staring over at Nevada and Taylor in shock and fear. Leslie looked like she wanted to say something, but didn't quite dare. Rosto was purposefully walking over from the computer into which he had no doubt just finished inputting Taylor's order.

"Either bite him or stop making a scene, Taylor," Rosto said boldly. He stopped walking a few feet away as if he couldn't quite make himself reach out to pull Taylor off.

Taylor took one last sniff before finally taking one step back from Nevada.

"He smells like a cat," Taylor explained.

Rosto nodded slowly. "I'm not surprised, given how many cats he rescues. Your food will be ready in a few minutes if you want to find somewhere to sit and wait. Nevada should get back to work."

Taylor nodded, frowning as he walked away from Nevada and Rosto. His tail wasn't wagging, but it wasn't tucked between his legs either. Nevada's own tail hadn't bottle-brushed at all, surprisingly. He didn't want to think about the mixed scents of wolf and clean soap that had gotten him to stay calm near a dog.

The chef must have rushed Taylor's sandwich because it appeared in a plastic to-go container a few moments later. Taylor left the restaurant after paying, and Nevada retreated to the back of the room to finally take his break. For the rest of his shift, his nose twitched whenever he thought he caught a hint of Taylor's scent again, though the day passed quickly enough. Nevada's thoughts were soon consumed with remembering orders and how much his feet hurt. The restaurant was as busy its second night as its first, and Nevada rushed around for hours ensuring everyone was happy and, as a result, his tips were large. He didn't have time to think about Taylor's behavior or what it might mean.

Nevada was waiting for the entire pack of wolves to come storming into the restaurant to throw him out of town, yet at the same time, the comfortable way Taylor had sniffed Nevada said the exact opposite. Nevada was a curiosity to Taylor whose only experience with cats might be Princess Pea, his grandfather's white ball of imperious fluff.

There had been scabs across Taylor's nose and cheeks, thin lines from kitten claws and teeth that would heal without scarring. Still, Taylor probably hadn't ever been attacked like that, so Nevada was also waiting for Taylor's revenge plot to hit and destroy him.

It was late when the restaurant finally closed and Nevada could go home. He had a feeling his hours might continue to change as they got a handle on the new restaurant. Rosto told him to arrive at eleven thirty the next morning to help open. Nevada wasn't looking forward to a third twelve-hour day in a row, but Rosto had promised both Nevada and Leslie a nice bonus in their paychecks that week for their extra hours, and he had put out an ad to hire more waitstaff.

Nevada was swimming in tip money anyway. He had more than enough to replace the aging cat tree and to buy himself plenty more expensive lox for his breakfast, but at the same time, he wanted to put the money away just in case he had to run from Taylor and his pack.

The usual chorus of meows greeted him when he walked into his apartment. Even Hex let out a growly meow, but he didn't leave his basket to come over to say hello so Nevada knew Hex was still angry he had been left home. After the obligatory petting and scratching, Nevada finally escaped into the bathroom for a quick wash before bed.

Showering never took long, but Nevada made sure to brush out all the tangles in his tail afterward. His tail was thicker and longer than a regular house cat's and had a lot more fur. He had a special cat brush that was able to dig in deep to really get the knots out. It felt good, and Nevada was purring softly to himself when he left the bathroom to crawl into bed.

Taylor was sitting on Nevada's floor in the center of the room. Beth and Maya were watching him closely from the nearest cat tree, and Hex lay on his back between Taylor's crossed legs. Hex was happily chewing on Taylor's fingers and batting at his wrist with sheathed claws as if they hadn't been snarling and attacking each other only a day ago. Taylor turned to look at Nevada as he walked out of the bathroom, and one blond eyebrow slowly lifted into the air.

Nevada gasped, a yowling sound that echoed slightly in his apartment, and jumped for his loft. He was naked with only the rosettes darkening his skin and his fur for cover. And that damned wolf had just seen him!

"What are you doing here?" Nevada snarled as he yanked his boxers on backward and carefully fit his tail through the hole. Once he was covered, he peered over the edge of his loft. Taylor was still idly playing with Hex under the other cats' watchful eyes, but his gaze was fixed on Nevada.

"Come down here, kitty, so we can talk," Taylor growled.

Nevada shook his head while lowering his body so only his eyes would be visible from the floor. Taylor might be playing nice at this moment, but he was a dog. His pleasant mood could easily vanish with the blink of an eye, and Nevada didn't want to be anywhere near him when it did. Except, the small part of him that remembered how nice Taylor had smelled and how warm his body had been pressed against Nevada's said the exact opposite. It was like his mind was getting pulled in two completely different directions. One side of him wanted to run and hide, certain he was about to get mauled horribly by a wolf, while the other wanted to roll in Taylor's scent like it was the purest of catnip.

"Get down here!" Taylor growled again, jolting Nevada out of his spinning thoughts. His voice was a touch deeper and more menacing than before. Nevada shook his head again, then had to hide a grin when Hex nipped Taylor's finger a little more sharply than previously, and Taylor yipped in surprised pain. "This is my territory, run by my pack," Taylor continued, his voice still in a low growl although he had lost a touch of his threatening tone thanks to Hex's complaint. "You are an interloper, like the hyenas, and I won't have that."

"I'm nothing like the hyenas!" Nevada protested. "I've been living here peacefully for three years without any problems. I've never blown anything up or hurt anybody." And he wanted to continue living his quiet life without the interference of annoying dogs. Unfortunately, he had a feeling that with his secret out in the open Taylor wasn't going to leave Nevada alone ever again.

"Allowing Ge-Mis that opportunity is an oversight I will be correcting as soon as this business with the damned hyenas has been taken care of. You are an oversight I can take care of right now. Get down here!"

Taylor probably didn't mean that he was going to kill Nevada; at least that's what Nevada hoped. Still, his words weren't exactly reassuring. Nevada didn't want to be run out of town or harassed by wolves until he had to leave to escape them. This was his home now, too, and he didn't want to go just because Taylor was in a snit.

"I'm not going anywhere," Nevada insisted. Leaving the home he had shared with his mother had been hard, one of the hardest things he had ever done. Their apartment hadn't been any larger than the one he had now, but Mom had made it home. With her gone, he couldn't stay there, and finding a new apartment by himself in that town just wasn't possible. The lord and lady had been true feudal rulers in the most clichéd sense: they owned everything and only allowed their tenants to live there on a case-by-case basis. Nevada hadn't wanted to expose himself to the amount of scrutiny moving to a new place would have required; it would have been much more in-depth than giving a bribe to Lord Reyes had been, and being found out as a Ge-Mi in that city would have been a death sentence. Nevada didn't know what would happen if Rosto or Lord Reyes found out, but their limited acceptance of Taylor hopefully meant it wouldn't be too bad.

Nevada didn't want to have to move to another city with another set of rules and have to figure out how hard hiding being a Ge-Mi was going to be. He couldn't allow

Taylor to push him out just because Taylor was a dog and Nevada a cat.

"It's not a request," Taylor growled. "Get down here now, or I'll come up and get you!"

Nevada didn't move his body, but his tail lifted in the air slightly and waved back and forth. He was taunting Taylor, but he couldn't help it. The wolf was barking up the wrong damned tree.

Taylor growled and pushed Hex to the side. Hex hissed and wandered off to his nest. Maya scooted after him with her own hiss at Taylor. Taylor ignored them both. He was backing up with his eyes fixed on Nevada. With a sudden snort he dashed forward at top speed and leaped with his hands outstretched to reach the loft. He missed by a mile and hit the ground with a thud.

Nevada scrambled forward to peer down from his loft to look at the crumpled heap of wolf groaning far below. He tried really hard to hold it in, but a snicker escaped, and once it did, Nevada couldn't help giggling helplessly.

"Shut up," Taylor growled, but there was more embarrassment and chagrin than anger in his voice. He pushed himself into a sitting position and shook himself from the tips of his red ears down through his red tail. "We are going to talk eventually. You can't hide behind Rosto or up there in your loft forever."

Nevada was certainly going to try.

Taylor stood with a grumble, and with one last scathing look over his shoulder up at Nevada, he stalked out Nevada's front door. He slammed the heavy wood shut behind him, and the tomcat yowled in surprise as he jumped awake and fell off his perch on a cat tree. Nevada counted to thirty slowly, then hopped down from his loft and scurried over to the door. He locked it, even though that wasn't enough deterrent to keep Taylor out, then hurried back up into his loft.

Apparently wolf Ge-Mis had the teeth, claws, speed, and hunting instinct of their fully animal brethren, but since wild wolves couldn't jump onto a high tree branch to hunt or escape a predator, the Ge-Mi version couldn't either. It was a relief to know Nevada could escape Taylor at any time simply by getting to a high location.

He managed to fall asleep quickly after that. Nevada didn't expect to, given how stressful his night had been, and he expected to have nightmares, too, but instead he woke up with a giggle at the memory of Taylor's miserable pout after he had failed to jump and snatch him. Nevada knew he shouldn't be laughing about it, that there would probably be consequences that would bite him in the butt at some point, but the amount of effort Taylor had put into his jump combined with his abject failure was too hilarious not to laugh over.

Despite his humor, Nevada kept an eye out during his walk to the café later that morning. He didn't want to get jumped simply because he wasn't being vigilant after Taylor's threats, but he didn't see anything unusual.

Rosto had finally hired a new waiter. Mary, "call me Ree," was shy and withdrawn. She definitely wasn't someone Nevada would have hired, based on her lackluster personality, but she worked hard in her third of the restaurant, and Nevada was only mostly exhausted instead of entirely by the time the restaurant closed its doors on their last customer.

"Good job today," Rosto said proudly as they all sat around one of the round tables to eat dinner. Ree smiled widely, her white teeth a brilliant contrast to her dark-skinned face, but didn't say anything. She hadn't said much to anyone except her customers all night. "I know it's tough work, and we're all on a learning curve, me included, but Lord Reyes is very pleased with how well the restaurant has been doing. He's given me leave to hire another waiter for the café, and I'm going to move one of my current staff over to the restaurant in the afternoon to help with the lunch rush. This means you three will have much more normal hours. Two of you will start coming in at three o'clock and will work until closing at eleven. One of you will come in for opening at eleven thirty, will work through the dinner rush, and leave at eight. Anyone have a preference?"

Ree shook her head wordlessly. Nevada shared a look with Leslie as they both thought it through. He honestly liked the idea of sleeping late in the morning and getting home at a normal hour.

"If Leslie doesn't mind, I'll take the earlier shift," Nevada said hopefully.

Leslie laughed. "I thought I'd have to fight you for the later shift! You think I want to be home in my empty apartment at night? This works fine for me, and you can go home and play with your cats."

Rosto nodded in agreement even as Nevada smiled a thank-you at Leslie for her understanding.

"I'll have a talk with Lord Reyes the next chance I get about hiring one more staff member to float hours so each of you can get some days off too. For now, please bear with it."

Nevada finished eating quickly once their conversation was done and headed home. There hadn't been a single sign or howl of a wolf all day. Neither Taylor nor his pack had stopped by, which Nevada hadn't expected. Taylor seemed so insistent, and his not showing up to bother Nevada was worrying. Either he had actually been hurt by his awkward fall, which Nevada doubted, or he was busy planning something awful. Nevada kept an extra careful eye on his surroundings and peeked cautiously into his apartment to see it was empty of all wolves before he walked inside to say hello to his cats.

A quick shower later and another wary peek out the bathroom door, with a towel wrapped around his waist, proved that the room was absent of wolves. Nevada really was starting to worry. He played with Hex for a while, yawning and glancing at the door with every creak of the building, and finally conceded that he needed to go to sleep if he wanted to be awake for work the next day.

Nevada tossed and turned for most of the night. His thoughts kept spinning, wondering what Taylor was up to, and every time the building shifted or noise from his neighbors filtered through the walls had him jumping. He finally fell asleep close to dawn and jolted awake a few hours later when his alarm of hungry cats yowled for their breakfast.

Answering the insistent call of hungry cats wasn't something he could ignore, so Nevada rolled out of bed, bleary-eyed and distinctly not bushy-tailed. He filled all the bowls with cat food and stuck his head into his fridge to see if he had anything easy to make tucked away in a back corner. In the end, he had toast with melted cheese on it and then regretted not thinking to add some canned tuna or salmon before he was finished eating.

His walk to work was again devoid of any wolves. Nevada's temperament turned quickly from anxiety to worry. Something had to be up. There was no reason for Taylor to actually stay away. Nevada felt jumpy all day. He startled every time the door swung open, which made Sing, the man Rosto had pulled from the café to work the lunch rush, look at Nevada strangely.

When Leslie and Ree came in, Nevada and Sing got their lunch break. Sing joined Nevada at the small table tucked next to the kitchen while they ate their sandwiches.

"What's up with you today?" Sing asked after a few minutes of silent eating.

Nevada didn't know how to answer that. Being worried about a Ge-Mi wasn't something he could really talk about.

"You know," Sing continued when Nevada didn't answer. "If I had a girlfriend or boyfriend that pushed me against a wall and started sniffing my neck, I'd expect to fall into bed for some great sex as soon as we were somewhere private. The way Reyes was sniffing you made me want to go find a nice wolf of my own. You sleeping with him?"

Nevada wordlessly shook his head, but the opening was too good to pass up. "He told me he would be back, but I haven't seen him in two days."

"So stop waiting for him to come to you. The wolves have a den right? Go see him."

Sing was probably right. Taylor had insistently invaded Nevada's territory. It wouldn't be too crazy to invade Taylor's in turn. Besides, the waiting and constant jumping every time the door opened was going to drive him nuts.

Decision made, Nevada nodded and smiled at Sing. "I'll do that. If I don't come in tomorrow, could you tell Rosto to send a rescue party?"

That made Sing laugh. "Should I warn him you might be naked and enjoying it?"

Nevada blushed, but didn't bother denying it. Sing didn't believe that Nevada wasn't sleeping with Taylor. Plus, there was a small part of Nevada that still remembered the way Taylor had smelled and how carefully he had been playing with Hex. That part didn't think it would be such a bad thing. Nevada quickly quashed that thought. Taylor was a nasty dog who was probably going to bite him for invading his territory. Nevada really needed the half of himself that kept trying to make him forget that all-important fact to shut up. Except, it was that part of him that was worried about

Taylor and had convinced him it was a good idea to search Taylor out.

What it really boiled down to in the end was Nevada needed to know what Taylor's real plans were. He couldn't take another night of not knowing and therefore not sleeping. He would have to confront Taylor tonight, and that was it.

With his decision made, Nevada returned to work. He just hoped Rosto really wouldn't have to send someone to rescue him in the morning.

Chapter Four

Taylor had set up his den within the city, so Nevada didn't have to walk far to reach it. He followed his nose and the rumors that he had heard over the years. Everyone knew which neighborhood to avoid if they wanted to stay off the wolves' radar, and it wasn't hard to identify which house belonged to the wolves from there: the large house smelled like Taylor and wolf. The Reyes mansion was just up the hill from Taylor's den, a constant reminder to Taylor and the rest of the city that the Reyes family ruled them.

Nevada hesitated, looking at the house Taylor's pack had claimed. This was one of the nicest neighborhoods in the city. Houses were large and sprawling. Each had about five acres of land that was thoroughly fenced in. The longest part of Nevada's walk had been going past all those fences. Now, he was dithering outside, trying to find the courage to go up to the front gate, press the intercom, and actually ask to talk to Taylor.

He was being ridiculous, Nevada decided. He was as much a predator as Taylor was, and this was the time to act like one.

Nevada strode forward quickly and reached out to touch the button on the gate that would announce his presence to those inside. Only, the button wasn't there. In fact, the entire DNA scanner had been ripped off the fence. The gate swung open with an easy push, and Nevada tentatively stepped through.

Taylor wasn't the type of person to destroy the technology that would keep his home and his pack safe. Something was wrong.

With his heart in his throat, Nevada hurried up the path to the front door. The house was closer to the street than most of the properties, which left an expansive backyard to run and play. Nevada was just glad he reached the door and the nearby window quickly. He peeked into the window and had to suppress a snarl.

The female wolf from the café, LeeAnne, Carley had called her, was lying in the front entry. She wasn't moving, and Nevada couldn't tell whether she was unconscious or dead. The lock and retinal scanner on the door were both broken. Nevada slowly pushed it open and carefully sniffed the air.

Hyenas. Their stench was unmistakable, as was the familiar cackle that filled the air.

"Idiot wolf," Nevada heard a woman saying through her laughter. "Sent your entire force out to search for the hyenas and left your den unprotected."

Nevada carefully peeked around the doorframe. Taylor was standing next to LeeAnne, his hands fisted at his sides and his teeth clenched on a growl. There were four hyenas standing between Nevada and Taylor. Nevada could only see their backs. The woman in the center was slightly closer to Taylor as she continued to taunt him. She had large, furry ears on top of her head, and her hair was brown with darker brown stripes through it. The man to her right wasn't wearing a shirt. His ears were smaller, and his body was covered in brown spots the same way Nevada's back was covered in rosettes. The two men to her left were fully clothed. One had legs that were too long to be fully human and appeared to be double-jointed at the knee. The other looked ordinary enough. He had the same large ears as the woman, but from the back Nevada couldn't see any other defining characteristics.

"So now we kill you, and when the rest of your pack arrives, we'll kill them too. The city will be ours, just as we were promised, and it won't be long before Lord Reyes is gone too. The rightful heir will take over." She finished speaking and took a threatening step toward Taylor. The three goons at her back let out yips of laughter as they also advanced.

Taylor was going to die, as was the rest of the pack. Nevada gritted his teeth and flexed his fingers. His claws were filed too short to be effective, but he wanted to rend and tear into the hyenas. They were the reason Nevada had to hide what he was. Their willingness to commit violence kept the humans scared of Ge-Mis like Nevada, who only wanted to live peacefully. Besides, he couldn't let them kill Taylor until after Nevada figured out the strange feelings Taylor was causing inside him.

Nevada quickly kicked off his shoes and socks so he could at least free the longer claws on his toes and then crept into the house on silent feet. Taylor noticed him at once, but Nevada could see him carefully keeping his face neutral so he didn't give Nevada's presence away. Nevada leaped high and pounced down on the female hyena's back, digging his claws in deep and scratching for all he was worth. Taylor went for the man to Nevada's right, closest to LeeAnne.

The woman screeched and reached for Nevada with her own claws, but Nevada jumped away. He landed on the banister of the nearby staircase, perching there and snarling down at the hyenas. Taylor also disengaged, leaving his victim unconscious on the floor.

"Who said I left my den unprotected?" Taylor taunted the hyenas. "Obviously, this was a trap to draw you in, and you fell for it. Clearly, you're not the brains. I don't think you're the brawn either. You're just a pack of stupid animals."

The female hyena snarled at Taylor's words, but there was blood pooling at her feet. Nevada had done some serious damage. Still, it was three versus two. The odds were in the hyenas' favor. Nevada could practically see the math running through her mind as she assessed Nevada and Taylor. She didn't appear surprised to see him there, but her focus was for Taylor, so maybe she didn't care about Nevada.

LeeAnne groaned. She opened her eyes slowly, saw the hyenas, and jumped to her feet with a growl. She wavered slightly, and she wasn't quite steady, but her claws were out, and she was ready to keep fighting.

Three against three and the blood was still dripping down the female hyena's back. The calculations abruptly changed, and without warning, she turned tail and ran out the door, the two men following on her heels. The fourth goon was left behind, bleeding and unconscious on Taylor's floor.

LeeAnne dropped back to the ground with a pained whine. Taylor reached into his pocket and pulled out his phone. He hit a few buttons and held it up to his ear, but his eyes were fixed on Nevada.

"The den was attacked," Taylor said sharply. "No, keep searching. We drove them off, and they're injured. See if you can sniff out the blood trail. Don't engage, just find them." He hit another button on his phone to hang up and then hit a speed-dial key. "The den was attacked," he repeated into the phone. "I need a medic for one wolf and someone to repair all the broken tech on the doors. Yes, Carley, I'm fine. Just send someone."

Taylor hung up again, and this time, he pocketed the phone. His blue eyes were burning, freezing Nevada in place on the banister with their intensity.

"Come on down, kitty," Taylor crooned. He took a step closer to Nevada, and Nevada tensed, ready to spring for the door and freedom. Taylor caught his movement and adjusted his steps to block that escape route. "I only want to talk."

"You're going to bite me," Nevada replied, but he hadn't looked away from Taylor's sharp gaze. "You're a dog; you're going to be mean."

Taylor tilted his head to the side as he contemplated Nevada's words. "You just saved my life, kitty. I don't think I would repay that by biting you. Although…" A grin flashed across his face for a brief moment that sent a surge of warmth down Nevada's spine to pool in his gut. Nevada's tail was still tucked against his knee, belying that he was agitated or upset with Taylor. "I could bite you. We would just have to be wearing less clothing at the time."

"Alpha, really?" LeeAnne groaned. "My head is spinning here, and even I can tell you're being an idiot."

Arousal pooled in his gut, sending a flush of heat to Nevada's face. Taylor finally looked away to give LeeAnne a worried once-over, and Nevada slipped from the banister to land soft-footed on the floor.

"There you are, kitty," Taylor said with another, less lascivious grin.

"My name is Nevada," Nevada said boldly.

Taylor's smile grew slightly. "Your hair is white like the snow of the Sierra-Nevada Mountains. I like it."

He had immediately guessed why Nevada's mother had named him Nevada. The knowledge made Nevada blush, which, in turn, made Taylor's tail wag. Taylor opened his mouth to say more, but the sound of a hover car's hydraulics setting down onto the pavement outside had him snapping his mouth shut again.

"What mess have you gotten yourself into this time, mutt?" Nevada didn't recognize the voice, but Taylor clearly did. He sighed heavily and rolled his eyes.

"The usual mess, barn-butt. Get in here and help LeeAnne." Taylor strode to the door as he spoke and pulled it all the way open.

An owl stepped into the house. Nevada had never seen an owl Ge-Mi before, but from the man's beak-like nose to the sharp eyes on his wide face and the feathers instead of hair on the top of his head, there was no other species he could be. He also had a stethoscope hanging around his neck. He swept Taylor and Nevada an assessing glance—no doubt seeing that while Nevada was covered in hyena blood, he didn't appear to be in any distress—before dismissing them both as perfectly healthy and hurrying past them to reach LeeAnne.

"That's Oliver. He's a barn owl," Taylor explained to Nevada. "He's a fully qualified doctor and one of the few willing to work on Ge-Mi patients. My grandfather hired him when my pack started patrolling the city."

"And he's saved your ass more times than I can count," Carley added as he stepped into the house. "Anyone else hurt?"

"LeeAnne and I were the only ones home when the hyenas broke in," Taylor explained. Carley nodded thoughtfully. He stepped past Taylor to kneel at the unconscious hyena's side. Carley reached into the bag he was holding and pulled out two sets of thick manacles that were connected by a few links of chain in the center. The first set went around the hyena's wrists, pulling his arms tight behind his back. The second went around his ankles, presumably to keep him from running away.

"Who bled all over the floor?" Carley asked once he was done. He brushed off his knees when he stood and then turned to look at Taylor. He caught sight of Nevada standing near Taylor, and one eyebrow lifted in surprise.

Taylor smoothly stepped between Carley and Nevada, blocking Carley's view of him. "The hyena leader. You have something to take samples with? I want to see if her DNA pops up on anyone's database. She essentially told me she was working for someone looking to unseat Grandpa from ruling this city. I'm hoping her DNA will let us track her movements before she was sent here. It might lead us to the culprit."

"It might," Carley said in agreement.

He dug into his bag again and pulled out what looked like a strange bit of paper. Except, Carley did something to the paper that made it start humming like a machine. He wiped the paper through the partially dried drips of blood, tucked the paper into a protective tube, and put the tube into his bag.

"I assume all the blood is hers," Carley continued, looking to one side. Nevada followed his gaze and winced. There were red footprints on the banister and on the floor below. Nevada looked down at his own feet and saw that they were bloody. "Which means we have Nevada to thank for your living hide, Taylor."

"Yeah, so?" Taylor asked aggressively.

Nevada suppressed a smile at how protective Taylor was being, but Nevada knew it was misplaced. Carley knew where Nevada worked and could even have Rosto bring Nevada somewhere to meet him without Taylor knowing. It would be far easier to get everything out in the open now.

"I was lucky," Nevada said over Taylor's growling. "I came to talk to Taylor at the right time. That's all." He stepped around Taylor so he was standing next to Taylor rather than behind him. Nevada reached up and carefully pulled the bandana off his head, revealing his ears. Carley didn't blink, which meant he had at least suspected what Nevada was even if he hadn't known outright. Instead, he looked at the way Taylor was hovering protectively and Nevada was firmly standing at Taylor's side, and smirked.

"We could use more of that luck," Carley finally replied. "And I know Lord Reyes would like to thank you personally. Taylor, help Nevada clean his feet so he can put his shoes and socks back on. Your grandfather is waiting for you."

Taylor growled, but obeyed. He reached out to take Nevada's hand in his and gently pulled Nevada farther into the house. Nevada clutched at Taylor's hand, surprised that the contact only inflamed the simmering lust still hiding just below the surface. Taylor hadn't bitten him, and Nevada had a feeling that Taylor would only chase him if they were playing a game where being caught would end pleasurably. Taylor was turning out to be the exact opposite of everything that had always scared Nevada about dogs. That, perhaps more than anything, was the reason Nevada held Taylor's hand tightly instead of screeching and jumping away.

They reached a nearby bathroom quickly, and Taylor led Nevada inside before closing the door behind them. The bathroom was as lavish as the rest of the house with a soaker tub, marble floors, and a marble countertop for the sink. Nevada sat down on the closed toilet while Taylor turned to get the water in the tub running.

"We do need to talk," Taylor murmured just loud enough for Nevada to hear over the running water. They were back to the conversation they had left off with Nevada safe in his loft and Taylor stuck far below. Except, this time, Taylor was testing the temperature of the water before gesturing that it was safe for Nevada to come wash off his feet.

Nevada carefully sat on the edge of the tub and swung his feet around so he could get them under the running water. He was sitting mere inches away from Taylor. "What do you want to talk about?"

Taylor laughed. "I'm not really sure anymore. You taunted me last time until I lost my temper and said things that were irrational and, quite frankly, impossible. I don't want to do anything to jeopardize the Ge-Mis in this city. About 25 percent of the population is Ge-Mi, and except for the damned hyenas, they live quietly. That's all that Grandpa asked for: they live quietly and pay their bribes. Until the hyenas came along, this was probably the city with the least confrontations between humans and Ge-Mis in the country."

"Then your grandfather knew what I am?" Nevada asked, honestly curious.

"When you gave him that damned cat? Not then. Three months later, Rosto was over for dinner, and he started telling stories about you. I think at the time you had rescued three kittens during your lunch break and had been trying to figure out how you were going to sneak them past Rosto until you could take them home that night."

"He found the kittens really quickly," Nevada said with a laugh, remembering the scene fondly even if, at the time, he had been terrified. "And then found a basket for them to sleep in safely for the rest of the day."

Taylor smiled. "He was trying to bribe us with funny stories into speaking with the health inspector about ignoring your cats in the café, but he got really serious a few seconds after he finished telling that story. I remember him saying, 'The kid finds cats absolutely everywhere and takes care of them until he can find them a home that is safe and happy. His giving you Princess Pea wasn't an insult at all. It was his way of saying that he believes your home is a good one where one of his precious cats can thrive.' Grandpa decided right then that you had passed your probationary period. I think he figured out that you're some type of cat Ge-Mi, from Rosto's stories."

"So you knew even before you broke into my apartment?" Nevada had to ask.

Taylor grinned at the memory, but shook his head. "I had no idea who Rosto was talking about at the time. It was three years ago, and I didn't connect the dots until I followed you home." Taylor laughed. "I hated you for a while, you know. You gave my grandfather that damned cat that keeps stealing my bed and my treats. It's like the cat lives to antagonize me, but Grandpa really likes her. She makes him happy and keeps him company, so I stopped hating you. I just wanted to steal a few of your treats and invade your life for a while."

"Just for a while?" Nevada paused scrubbing between his toes so he could hear Taylor's answer.

Taylor was quiet for a long moment, his blue eyes hooded as he stared blindly at the wall behind Nevada. "Maybe for longer," he said gently, refocusing on Nevada with new intensity in his eyes. "I don't know you well enough yet to say more."

Which was about where Nevada was. Taylor hadn't bitten or snarled at Nevada, and he appeared to be a nice guy. For a dog, at least. It was as good a place as any to start a relationship.

Nevada quickly finished washing the blood off his feet and took the towel Taylor handed him to dry off. They headed back to where Carley was waiting. LeeAnne and the hyena were both gone from the foyer. Carley saw them both immediately and gestured that they should follow him out to the car. His eyes didn't even pause when he saw Nevada's still-exposed ears. They stopped briefly for Nevada to gather his abandoned footwear.

"The crew to fix all your scanners and locks are on their way," Carley explained to Taylor over his shoulder while they waited. "I have people watching the house until it's secured again." Nevada finished putting on his shoes, and they resumed walking to the car.

The driver hurried to open the doors so they could all climb into the back. Nevada followed Taylor inside and took a seat. A few moments later, the car gently bounced into the air and began flying up the hill toward the Reyes mansion. They were silent for the few short minutes, but Nevada could feel Taylor's warmth. It comforted him. With Taylor there, as scary as it was to be dragged before Lord Reyes, nothing too bad could happen.

Once they arrived at the mansion, Carley led them through a private entrance and into hallways that Nevada knew he shouldn't have ever been given access to: the private domain of the Reyes family. It was as opulent as the meeting room from Nevada's memory. The fancy cloth wallpaper was painted white with molding cut into ornate shapes along the ceiling. Each doorway they passed was built of beautiful dark wood that only emphasized how much money this family had.

It was pretty damn intimidating, but neither Taylor nor Carley seemed to notice the beauty as they walked past. They went up a flight of stairs eventually, each step built of shining marble, and finally turned into a sitting room at the top of the stairs.

Lord Reyes didn't look any different than Nevada remembered. He was sitting in a large chair, a delicate-looking cup of tea held in one hand. He carefully put the cup back on the waiting saucer on the table before standing.

"Taylor, I heard you encountered a difficulty. I assume you're all right?" His words sounded stiff and formal, but the way his very blue eyes—the same shade as Taylor's—carefully inspected Taylor from head to toe said otherwise.

Taylor sighed heavily, snorting through his nose, and collapsed into a chair across the table from Lord Reyes.

"Damned hyenas," Taylor grumbled. "They knew where my den was and had someone watching it to know when all my wolves were out on patrol."

"They didn't follow one of your wolves home?" Lord Reyes asked sharply. He hadn't returned to his seat, and Nevada didn't dare follow Taylor's example and take his own seat.

"My wolves haven't been home in two days. The house has been empty, and we've been denning wherever we could find at night. LeeAnne and I stopped in to check if Carley had left any messages and to charge our phones. Not even five minutes later, the hyenas broke through the front door."

"So someone must have told the hyenas. Who knew Taylor's address?" Lord Reyes asked Carley. This time his eyes matched the sharpness in his voice.

"Too many people," Carley replied with a heavy sigh of his own. "I'll start looking into it, but I think we'll get more out of the hyena we've captured and the blood sample we were able to collect from the hyena leader."

"See that it's done, Carley," Lord Reyes said. He smiled at Carley, which softened his words and made him seem less imperious and more like he was asking for a favor.

Carley smiled back. "I'll get on it right now." He bowed slightly before turning and hurrying from the room. He closed the door behind him, leaving Nevada alone with Taylor and his grandfather.

Princess Pea wormed her way out from beneath the cushions on the long couch and stretched out with a loud yawn that showed off her teeth. She dug her claws into the cushion a few times as she studied the people around her. Nevada could see her indecision as she tried to decide if she wanted petting from Lord Reyes or whether she wanted to taunt Taylor instead. Then, she caught sight of Nevada standing awkwardly by the doorway and shot off the cushion toward him with a loud yowl. Pea jumped into his arms with a cry and snuggled close.

She was soft, as if she had been brushed recently, and her coat gleamed with health. Nevada gratefully buried his face in her fur and hugged her.

"Please, sit, Nevada," Lord Reyes said gently.

Nevada peeked through Pea's fur to see Lord Reyes stifle a small smile. With Pea still curled in his arms, Nevada sank down on the couch she had just vacated.

"It would seem your timing tonight was quite fortuitous," Lord Reyes continued once Nevada was settled. "Why were you headed to Taylor's?"

Nevada knew what he was really asking. How had Nevada known where Taylor's supposedly secret den was located?

"I followed my nose," Nevada explained. "Taylor's scent is all over the city, but it's concentrated near the areas he spends the most time. It's how he found my home, so I used my nose to find his."

"Could that be how the hyenas found you, Taylor?" Lord Reyes asked.

"I don't know how strong a hyena's nose is," Taylor admitted, "but I'll ask Carley after we're done here."

They lapsed into silence for a few moments that was only broken by Princess Pea's purring. Lord Reyes studied Nevada, but Nevada didn't know what he was looking for. Taylor appeared to be waiting for his grandfather to take the lead, although he also kept giving Nevada reassuring smiles whenever he caught Nevada looking at him.

"Well, whatever the reason you were headed to Taylor's house, I do appreciate the fact that you saved his life. We've had a difficult few months..."

"More than a few months," Taylor interrupted with a hard laugh.

"True enough," Lord Reyes agreed easily. He didn't explain further, instead taking a few minutes to watch Nevada, who tried not to squirm under the attention.

"Someone tried to kill Grandpa," Taylor finally jumped in, apparently impatient for the conversation to continue.

"Taylor!" Lord Reyes scolded immediately.

"What? The only iffy thing about Nevada is he smells like cats, and it's growing on me. He's not working for the cousins," Taylor said earnestly to his grandfather.

"How can you be certain?" Lord Reyes replied, but from the tone of his voice, Nevada thought he was testing Taylor rather than reprimanding him.

"Rosto's certain," Taylor said. "And he doesn't smell like deceit. Besides, I like him."

Nevada flushed red at that and hid his face in Pea's fur again.

Lord Reyes turned toward Nevada, apparently satisfied with Taylor's rationalization, and began explaining.

"About a year and a half ago someone poisoned me with a rare form of snake venom we can only assume was harvested from a Ge-Mi. Thanks to an excellent staff of doctors, I survived with all my faculties intact. However, it was clear to me and to Taylor that this was merely the first salvo in the war. Assassinating me before Taylor was able to fully take on the responsibilities of running this city would leave Taylor greatly weakened.

"Since then, we have been working to strengthen our position and to ferret out whoever is behind this. Taylor has taken on much of the leadership duties he had previously been neglecting and has slowly been proving his worth as a man, rather than as a Ge-Mi, to this city. All the while we have been working to discover who our enemy is. We believe it is a child or grandchild of one of my two siblings, which narrows the list down to seven people."

"There's a rumor in the city that you're sick, Lord Reyes," Nevada said softly. "Is that because you were poisoned?"

Lord Reyes's smile was grim. "The rumor was spread by whoever poisoned me, but we have been trying to take full advantage of it. Taylor has become the leader of this city in my absence, and people have started to become used to him. When I am gone, in truth, Taylor should have little issue keeping power. Plus, those who want to take advantage of the fact that I am ill have started to build their coup, which will hopefully allow us to track them and stop them."

"The hyenas were brought into the city by someone," Taylor added. "And we're hoping to find out who and finally put an end to this mess."

Nevada appreciated the explanation, but why were they telling him all of this? Apparently, they trusted him, which was nice to know, but Lord Reyes could have simply thanked him for saving Taylor rather than giving him the full explanation. They wanted him for something.

"Where do I fit into all this?" Nevada had to ask.

Lord Reyes's smile at Nevada's words was very appreciative. He liked that Nevada hadn't simply rolled over and let them rope him into whatever their scheme was.

"The simplest way to explain it is that you've involuntarily gotten yourself involved," Lord Reyes said.

"You protected Taylor Reyes from the hyenas. They have seen your face and your uniform, which means they know where to find you. You are now a target they will no doubt try to silence, and we will be waiting to take them down."

Nevada looked down at his uniform in sudden horror. The Café Spice logo was embroidered on the breast pocket, which meant the hyenas could right now be bombing the building.

Lord Reyes no doubt saw the worry on Nevada's face because he continued quickly. "We have time to prepare. We have captured one of the hyenas, which means they're down strength, and you seriously injured their leader. In the time it takes them to regroup, we will be ready for them. Rosto has already been warned."

"What about my apartment building?" Nevada asked. "It's not exactly secure, and all my cats live there."

"The security has already been upgraded. Carley sent someone there as soon as he realized the hyenas might retaliate."

"Plus," Taylor added, "I'll go home with you tonight and watch your back."

"I'm not sure Beth will allow that," Nevada admitted, although he did feel better about the idea.

Taylor shrugged. "Hex likes me. He'll tell her to let me in."

"Hex tried to bite your nose off," Nevada said, laughing at the disgruntled expression that briefly crossed Taylor's face.

"We've come to an understanding about that," Taylor said. His expression was pointedly blank, but Nevada could see his eyes swimming with laughter. Nevada couldn't help grinning back.

"I'm glad that's settled," Lord Reyes cut in before Nevada could taunt Taylor some more about it. The levity in the room immediately vanished, and both Nevada and Taylor turned back toward Lord Reyes. "Nevada, you may be asked to stand at Taylor's side as a Ge-Mi in front of the entire city. Do you think that might be something you could do?"

He had been hiding all his life out of necessity. Ge-Mis were ostracized and outright killed if they weren't careful. Yet, Taylor's continued existence proved that this city was different—or could be. Nevada could uncover his ears and let his tail out, and only a few humans would take issue. Those humans would be asked to leave the city, not Nevada, thanks to Lord Reyes.

What really worried Nevada, however, was the fact that someone wanted to take the city from Lord Reyes, and there was no guarantee the new lord would be as willing to allow Ge-Mis. Certainly Nevada would be forced to leave, thanks to his association to Taylor. Nevada would have to do everything he could to help Lord Reyes stay in power just for his own happiness. Whatever he was starting to build with Taylor was a different issue altogether, but at the same time, it wasn't.

Was he willing to stand at Taylor's side, not only as a Ge-Mi, but also as Taylor's mate? The answer to the first part was yes. Nevada already knew he'd throw everything he had into helping the Reyes family stay in power, which would in turn help every Ge-Mi in the city. Nevada didn't have an answer to the second part of the question just yet.

Lord Reyes apparently didn't want an answer at the moment because he stood and headed toward the door.

"Let me get a driver to bring you back down to the city," he said to them both before turning to Taylor specifically. "I'll have Oliver give you a call once he's finished evaluating LeeAnne. Call in your wolves for a pack meeting tomorrow; Carley will have new instructions for you and the results of the DNA test. Until then, stay close to Nevada." He turned back to Nevada. "Thank you again for saving my grandson. I owe you a large favor. Is there anything you need?"

Nevada hesitated a moment before deciding to go for it. "I have a tomcat that is looking for a good home..."

A startled shout of laughter escaped Lord Reyes, and he had to brace one hand on the wall to catch himself.

"I'll see what I can do," he promised. "Taylor, make sure Nevada stays safe. I like him."

Taylor grinned. "I like him, too, but I saw him first, so hands off."

Lord Reyes laughed again. "Get out of here, scamp."

Taylor went, but he waited in the hall for Nevada to gently pet Princess Pea one last time before handing her over to Lord Reyes. Then, Nevada bowed to Lord Reyes before hurrying after Taylor.

Chapter Five

Nevada found a new scanner on the front door to his apartment. It was top-of-the-line, hard to fool, and a good way of keeping people who didn't belong in the building out. Nevada scanned his fingerprint, felt the brief bite of the DNA checker, and the door unlocked with a click.

Taylor opened the door for him and then led the way up the stairs to Nevada's front door. The tech there was also improved with a retinal scanner as well as the usual physical lock that Nevada had to dig his key out to open.

A chorus of "hungry, feed me now" meows greeted them as Nevada pushed the door open. The cats fell silent when they saw Taylor except for Beth's drawn-out hiss of disapproval.

"He's staying here tonight," Nevada explained. He could feel the air of condemnation in the room grow heavier at his words. Then, Hex bounced into the open. He stalked to Taylor and meowed imperiously until Taylor bent to scratch him behind the ears.

Nevada left Hex to keep Taylor distracted while he swiftly filled food bowls. A yawn caught Nevada as he was putting down the last bowl. The adrenaline had begun to wear off, the long day finally catching up with him.

"I need to shower," Nevada said. "Don't destroy anything."

Taylor grinned but nodded. He sat on the floor with Hex climbing across his lap, happy to tease the kitten with his fingers. Hopefully, he would stay there, but Nevada still hurried into the bathroom.

His showers were usually short—he didn't want to stay in the water any longer than he had to—but Nevada didn't think he had ever taken one so quickly before. He wrapped a towel around his waist and grabbed his brush before heading back into the main room.

Taylor hadn't moved. Hex was stubbornly clinging to the front of Taylor's shirt, but Maya was meowing at him. Her food bowl was empty, and it was apparently time for Hex to have dinner as well.

"What does she want?" Taylor asked Nevada. He didn't turn away from Maya, who was puffed up and very angry-looking, but Nevada saw his eyes cut sideways toward him.

"She wants to feed Hex, and he's refusing to leave you," Nevada replied. He took a firm grip on the towel and jumped, landing safely in his loft where he could quickly scramble into a clean pair of boxers.

Taylor started detangling Hex from his shirt. Nevada saw how careful he was not to hurt Hex even as Hex started thrashing unhappily. It wasn't long before Maya had a sulking Hex in her teeth. She carried him away to his nest of blankets, and Taylor finally looked up at Nevada.

"I'm going to need to get a ladder in here," Taylor said with a grumpy pout.

"I have a ladder," Nevada replied with a smirk, "but I'm not going to let you up here like that."

"Like what?" Taylor asked, frowning unhappily.

Nevada paused a moment to school his face and then said, "Smelling like a gutter dog." He didn't want to laugh too hard, although he was definitely giggling slightly as he spoke. "There are fresh towels in the closet. Go shower, and I'll think about letting you up."

The alternative was taking apart his careful configuration of blankets and pillows to give a few to Taylor to sleep on. Nevada wanted to do that even less than he wanted to invite a dog into his home. Although, Nevada had to admit that inviting Taylor into his apartment hadn't really been that difficult. Was he, instead, really looking for an excuse to invite Taylor into his bed? Nevada quashed that thought before it could grow any further.

Taylor sniffed his arm briefly and then sighed. "I'll shower," he grumped, "but you better be telling the truth about the ladder." Nevada waited until the bathroom door closed behind Taylor before going over to the far side of his loft and kicking down the ladder. It was made of rope and wood with red-painted steps attached by knotted lengths of rope. Flimsy didn't even begin to describe it, but the previous owner had installed it securely enough.

From the floor, Nevada could pull it down with a broom handle, but since he preferred jumping, he didn't bother with it most days.

The shower shut off a few minutes later. Nevada busied himself with his brush, trying to get all the tangles out of his tail. Taylor came out of the bathroom smelling like Nevada's shampoo, which was infinitely better than how he had smelled before. The ladder creaked as he pulled himself up, and Nevada was glad to see he was also wearing boxers, although his had a normal hole in the front and an extra one sewn into the back for his tail. He caught sight of Nevada pulling the brush through his tail and grinned.

"Let me help," Taylor said, holding out his hand for the brush. Nevada figured he only wanted to get his own tail untangled, but Nevada handed over the brush anyway. Taylor, instead, reached for Nevada's tail. He held it gently despite its heft—a snow leopard's tail was thicker than any other cat's—and slowly stroked the brush deep into Nevada's fur.

Nevada let out an involuntary purr and arched his back at the wonderfully massaging feel of those bristles digging deep. Taylor chuckled, but just pulled the brush through a second and third time. Nevada relaxed into the pillows and blankets beneath him, purring softly, and Taylor continued to brush until Nevada was a giant kitty puddle.

Nevada almost didn't notice when one of Taylor's hands gently stroked his ears, but his body noticed immediately. His purr went deeper, into his chest, and Taylor let out a low rumble of his own at the sound. Taylor stopped brushing Nevada's tail, but his hand continued to stroke along Nevada's ears.

How long had it been since someone had touched him so gently, especially on the parts of him that were blatantly nonhuman? Nevada couldn't remember. His mother had when he was a child mewling for comfort, but she had stopped when he started growing up. Everyone else thought he was human, and he wouldn't have let them touch him anyway. This type of comfort was therefore foreign to him, yet still so welcoming at the same time.

Taylor's hand drifted down from Nevada's head, following the trail of fur that covered his spine. His fingertips circled some of the black rosettes, tracing their shape and sending a shiver through Nevada's body that had the tip of his tail twitching. Taylor chuckled, his voice as low as Nevada's purrs.

"I never thought I would think a cat beautiful," Taylor murmured softly into one of Nevada's small ears. He nipped lightly at the short fur there with his sharp teeth, and Nevada jumped with a yowl of surprise.

"You bit me!" Nevada gasped. He rolled onto his side to look at Taylor, only realizing as he moved that the air in the room had suddenly changed.

Taylor was holding back laughter. He pressed his lips together tightly, but his eyes said he found Nevada utterly hilarious.

"Sorry," Nevada said. He had ruined whatever it was Taylor was trying to do; the pleasant lethargy that had enveloped him a moment before had vanished.

"Don't be sorry," Taylor replied immediately, although his voice was still light with laughter. "I forgot that you've been in hiding for so long. You have zero experience."

He didn't say it like that was a bad thing, so Nevada decided not to be offended. Still, it wasn't pleasant to hear what he had missed out on.

The brush had dropped onto the blankets at some point. Nevada picked it up and then looked at Taylor, unsure how he should ask if it was okay. Taylor apparently understood as he turned around slightly so Nevada had access to his tail. The bright-red fur had started to dry, and it was knotted. Nevada had to be a bit more forceful with the brush than Taylor had been, but every time Nevada looked up in apology, Taylor was smiling slightly and didn't seem upset with the pulled fur in the least.

It was like Nevada was looking at a different man. This wasn't the Taylor who had angrily and stubbornly jumped for the loft. Yet, at the same time, there was still the same level of stubbornness in the way Taylor was determinedly wooing Nevada.

Nevada had no idea how to respond. Absolutely none. Instead, he focused on getting every last knot out of Taylor's tail before it could start matting.

"It's okay, kitty," Taylor said. His voice was gentle, as was his smile, but there was an edge to it that brought back that tight feeling in Nevada's gut. "Let's just go to sleep tonight. We'll figure everything else out after we've handled the hyenas."

Nevada ran the brush through Taylor's tail one more time, satisfied when it moved smoothly without hitting any tangles. The brush itself had a mixture of Nevada's white fur and Taylor's red. It was pretty, but Nevada knew he was only staring at it to stall. Taylor apparently knew too. He took the brush from Nevada's hand and put it aside, then dug in the blankets by their feet—where Nevada had carelessly kicked them just the previous morning—until he found the fluffy comforter. He pulled it up over his legs, and then he lifted one eyebrow at Nevada as if asking whether Nevada was going to lie down or not. Nevada did, curling up in the many pillows that comprised his nest, and Taylor tugged the blanket up to their chins. Nevada groped over his head until he found the light switch, and the room went dark.

"Good night, kitty," Taylor said through a yawn. Nevada could feel him sprawled out across much of Nevada's nest, apparently perfectly comfortable, and within a few short minutes, his breathing evened out into sleep.

"Good night," Nevada whispered back. He was convinced he wouldn't be able to sleep with Taylor so close, but the long day caught up with him quickly. Nevada closed his eyes and sleep overcame him.

*

The usual griping of hungry cats demanding breakfast, which was Nevada's normal alarm clock, was absent when Nevada slowly began to drift awake. It took him a moment to realize this was a bad thing. He sat up with a gasp of worry and crawled quickly to the edge of the loft. A peek over the edge showed Taylor filling the last bowl with food and contented cats munching happily away.

"You're awake," Taylor called when he caught sight of Nevada. He smiled up at Nevada, and a jolt hit Nevada right in the chest. Nevada could only nod wordlessly before rolling over to dig out a pair of sweatpants and a T-shirt from the drawers along the back wall. Once he was dressed, Nevada jumped down from the loft. Taylor was sprawled on the floor again with Hex crawling all over him. The rest of the cats, Beth and Maya included, had chosen to finish their breakfast instead of keeping a careful eye on Taylor's every move. That amount of trust wasn't something Nevada had expected from any of his cats this quickly, but they had apparently decided Hex was safe with Taylor.

"You want food?" Nevada asked. He was feeling shy and couldn't quite look Taylor in the eye. He glanced up and saw Hex hanging upside down in the air, clinging by his claws to the sleeve of Taylor's shirt. Nevada laughed with Taylor, and just like that, Hex had broken the ice. He hurried to the fridge and got out his usual breakfast of bagels with cream cheese and lox. With Hex still hanging from his arm, Taylor came over to help. Since lox was Nevada's favorite, he was happy to see Taylor bite into his bagel without hesitation.

They ate slowly, Nevada savoring every bite of the sharp fish. Hex followed his nose until Taylor had to fend him off to keep his bagel safe. It was almost time to wean Hex and get him eating solid food, and Hex was apparently willing to take matters into his own claws. He yowled unhappily from the floor where Taylor put him when it became clear that Hex wasn't going to give up on getting some fish. Taylor's next bite of bagel and lox was almost savage, and the gleam in his eyes told Nevada he was enjoying tormenting Hex, who finally huffed and stalked off into the mess of cat trees under the loft.

Nevada couldn't think of anything to talk about, although they had hours to fill before he went to work. His mind drifted back to their conversation the previous night, which reminded him that he had been purring in Taylor's lap like he was in heat. Nevada forced those thoughts away before his face turned red and Taylor noticed the direction his brain had gone. Instead, he thought back to earlier in the night, to when the hyenas had brazenly attacked Taylor.

"Were the hyenas really going to kill you?" Nevada asked.

Taylor paused with the bagel halfway to his mouth. He put the bagel back on his plate and frowned thoughtfully for a long moment.

"I think so," Taylor finally replied, "but I've been thinking about it, too, and now I'm not sure. They busted in and got LeeAnne quickly. I came running, but instead of taking me out right then, they stopped to gloat."

"Were they stalling?" Nevada couldn't help wondering.

"They rushed it with LeeAnne. They only knocked her out when I'm sure they would have preferred to kill her," Taylor mused. "You're correct that something doesn't seem right, but I couldn't even start to guess what they were stalling for."

"I guess my arrival messed with those plans though," Nevada said. He shrugged, willing to let the speculation fade, so they could move to a different topic. Taylor didn't notice Nevada's intentions, focused inward on some thought.

"What if your arrival was part of their plan?" Taylor stated sharply, looking up at Nevada with a wild gleam in his eyes. "What would have happened when Carley came to the house? We were supposed to meet with him that night but had come early to change clothes and charge our phones. He would have seen the broken tech on the gate and then found my body and you leaning over me. Everyone would assume you had a hand in the attack, and since Rosto has been adamant about supporting you all these years, it would have cast suspicion on him. The entire network of people Grandpa and I know that we can trust would have been thrown into complete upheaval. Our whole operation to stop whoever is trying to throw the coup would have been destroyed. Without me to support him, Grandpa would have lost everything in hours."

"But who knew that I was even planning to go to your den, let alone when?" Nevada had to ask, unable to completely agree with Taylor's assessment. Yet, he also couldn't help remembering the conversation he'd had with Sing, and how Sing had convinced Nevada to go visit Taylor at his den. "It's not me Rosto needs to worry about. It's Sing," Nevada realized. "Sing is the one who told me to go find you. He knew when my shift ended too." He was one of the new hires Rosto had rushed to get with the expansion to the restaurant. How closely had Rosto checked their backgrounds? Nevada didn't want to complain though, because Rosto hadn't checked Nevada's background closely either. And that was something Nevada was thankful for.

"If so, they were able to sneak someone inside," Taylor said through a growl. He stuffed the last bite of bagel into his mouth and chewed hard, as if he could take his frustrations out that way. "I need to make some phone calls, see what our next move should be," Taylor added once he had swallowed. "I'll be back to walk you to work."

He put his plate in the sink and ran his fingers gently over Nevada's ears as he walked behind Nevada's chair. Nevada couldn't help screeching in surprise, but by the time the shiver of shock and want had worked its way through his spine and out his tail, Taylor's happy laughter was the only part of him remaining. The front door closed and locked automatically behind him, but they both knew that wouldn't keep Taylor out.

Nevada let out a heavy sigh, trying to figure out what it all meant. With Taylor gone, he could return to the feelings he had been putting off. Nevada knew what want felt like. The human half of his reproductive system worked fine, even if he had only experimented with it on his own. Yet, that wasn't what had happened last night. He hadn't been hard or ready to mate; he had been a purring puddle instead. Taylor had managed to relax every single one of Nevada's barriers with a simple hairbrush. It was frightening, but at the same time exhilarating. But, when Taylor's hands had started touching his ears, Nevada's thoughts started to turn more human and carnal.

Was that also true of Taylor? Had the bite not been an admonishment, but rather a wolf's way of saying he was interested too? It was clear that Taylor had considerably more experience in the area than Nevada and that Taylor was more than willing to go slow until Nevada's inexperienced brain eventually caught up.

Nevada would catch up. He wanted to know where these strange feelings that had turned Taylor from an icky dog into a sexy wolf would eventually lead them. He had a feeling he would enjoy the experience immensely and that Taylor would hold on to Nevada tightly forever if Nevada let him.

The truth was, Nevada did want to let Taylor in. He wouldn't have lowered the ladder last night if he didn't, but it was also true that Nevada was going to be acting on instinct alone until he figured out where there was stable ground in their rocky relationship.

It would have to be enough for them both. It still felt strange to so suddenly shift his mind view of Taylor, but Nevada would hold on tightly with both hands until he had it figured out. He knew Taylor would be there the entire time.

With that settled, Nevada took a deep breath and then finished the last of his bagel. A glance at the clock told him there was still a lot of time before he had to leave. There were litter boxes to clean, so Nevada put his own plate in the sink to deal with later and went to find a trash bag and the scoop.

Chapter Six

Taylor received stares everywhere he went, and by extension, people also stared at Nevada because he was walking next to Taylor. Nevada had tucked his tail and ears away like usual, so he looked human enough, but regular people didn't walk through the city next to Taylor Reyes. Hex had unhappily stayed home, so Nevada didn't have to worry about him today.

Luckily the walk to the café was quick. Nevada went in the restaurant half and found Rosto and Carley waiting for them.

"You're sure it was Sing," Rosto said softly once Nevada and Taylor were close enough to hear.

"Sing told Nevada to come find me, which is when the trap was sprung," Taylor replied.

Rosto and Carley looked at Nevada for confirmation, so he nodded to show that Taylor was telling the truth.

"Damn," Rosto hissed out between his teeth. "I can't believe I missed him."

"Could be he was recruited after you hired him," Carley said placatingly. "I started a background check on him last night, but he hasn't lived in Kensey for very long. It's much harder to get information from his previous cities, so it'll take a while longer."

"What about the hyenas?" Taylor asked.

Carley sighed. "It's mostly the same issue. The hyena we captured and the blood sample both lead to Morse, which doesn't tell us much. Hyena noses are as strong—if not stronger—than a wolf's, so trying to identify who might have given them the address to your den is a dead end. Unfortunately, all we have right now from that encounter is the fact that Nevada injured their leader, and one of her lieutenants is in our custody."

"But we can talk to Sing now," Rosto added with a growl. "Let me discreetly grab him." Rosto walked off to the archway between the two halves of the building. Carley seemed content to wait, but Nevada had a few questions.

"What's Morse?" he asked first.

Taylor sighed. "It's a city to our west. After the wars, powerful families or coalitions took control of all the cities, but there are a few left with no leader. Either there isn't anyone strong enough to take power or the leader was killed and left behind a power vacuum no one has been able to fill. Towns like that are lawless and usually rife with Ge-Mi and human gangs fighting to become the new leaders. Morse is one of those cities. It's usually a dead end when we track someone there unless we get lucky and find the trail that led them to the city in the first place."

"But we've gotten very good at finding that trail over the years," Carley added smugly. "We'll find out where those hyenas came from."

"Could you also track the seven people on your coup list to see if they might have sent someone to Morse to hire the hyenas?" Nevada asked. Carley and Taylor immediately smiled as if they were impressed.

"Already done, but good idea," Carley said. "You're too smart to be working in a restaurant the rest of your life. Come work for me instead."

"No poaching my best employee!" Rosto barked as he rejoined them. Sing was with him, looking bewildered.

"Lord Reyes has a few questions for you, Sing," Carley said, almost gently. His words immediately had Sing tensing, but had someone said the same thing to Nevada a day ago, he would've had the same reaction. It wasn't an expression of guilt, just worry. "Let's take a seat over here and talk." Carley waved to a table hidden in the back of the restaurant and then herded Sing toward one of the chairs.

"Let Carley work his magic," Rosto said with a sigh. "Nevada, we still need to get the restaurant ready for opening. Taylor, one of your wolves is across the street, probably looking for you."

Taylor nodded and left, but not before smiling quickly at Nevada. Nevada let the automatic shiver run through his body, swiftly getting used to the odd feelings of want Taylor inspired, and then he went to start organizing the table waiting list for that night.

Nevada couldn't help noticing that Sing openly sobbed as Carley spoke with him. He also didn't deny anything Carley was accusing him of. Nevada almost wanted to feel bad for him, but Sing had tried to set him up for Taylor's murder. He couldn't feel any remorse.

"I can't. My mother—"

"Is of no concern to us," Carley snapped, cutting off Sing's desperate plea mid word.

"She's sick!" Sing insisted. "Moving to another city would kill her."

Rosto drifted over to the table as if he thought Sing might get violent and Carley could use some help. He didn't need to bother as another look at Carley's hard and unforgiving expression caused Sing to dissolve into more tears.

Nevada couldn't simply watch any longer. Three years ago, he would have been the one sitting in that chair, his mother dying of illness and him desperate for any help to get her healthy again. It was only because his mom had insisted he not do anything foolish that Nevada hadn't met any unsavory types trying to save her. On the days he missed her the most, he regretted obeying her. Had she survived another month, Nevada's life might be very different. He could see himself in Sing's slumped shoulders and heavy tears.

Rosto was standing behind Sing's chair waiting for direction from Carley, who looked like his patience was quickly coming to an end.

"What did they bribe you with?" Nevada asked.

Sing looked up in surprise, but Carley answered scathingly. "Money, which he claims to have spent on doctor's visits for his sick mother. His story sounds a little too altruistic to be real in my opinion."

Nevada saw Sing's last bit of hope break as his eyes darkened, and his lips quivered with more tears.

"Can't you make a few calls to see if he's telling the truth?" Nevada asked. "You must have spies all over the city; someone must be able to verify his story."

"Why?" Carley asked Nevada sharply. "He's a traitor to the Reyes family. He'll be lucky to be alive tomorrow. Why should I waste my resources on him?"

"Sing," Nevada said in a softer voice, turning to look at Sing as he spoke, "who bribed you exactly? Was it the hyenas?"

Sing shook his head wordlessly. He was shaking in his chair as the enormity of what he had gotten involved with had finally struck home.

"Man," he forced out. "It was a m-man. I h-have a picture on my ph-phone. W-wanted to know what I was g-getting into. D-didn't know it was th-this bad until they t-told me to talk to Nevada."

"You thought you were just their eyes inside Rosto's domain?" Carley asked with a raised eyebrow.

Sing nodded. "Didn't t-tell them much. Not much to tell." He glanced around the shop and shrugged. Nevada knew what he was saying: Rosto might be good friends with the Reyes family, but he didn't conduct any plotting in the restaurant. Not much happened here at all, except for Taylor Reyes suddenly showing an interest in one of Rosto's waiters.

"With whom did you speak?" Carley asked. "How did you pass on your information?"

"I'll t-tell you everything," Sing insisted. "Just, when you execute me, please, my m-mother. Make sure she gets better?"

"That's what you want in exchange for your information?" Carley asked, sounding surprised. He stood from his chair suddenly, the scrape of the legs against the floor grating and startling after the last few intense minutes. "If your story clears and you really do have a sick mother, I'll see she's given the best care possible. Your own life depends on a few things. First, I want to know what information you have about your blackmailers. After that, we'll talk. If you can prove your worth to the Reyes family, you might just live. Show me your phone."

Sing nodded jerkily and carefully stood. He was still shaking as he led the way into the kitchen and toward the lockers where some of the staff kept their personal items during their shifts.

"Oh, Nevada," Rosto sighed heavily. He shook his head slightly as if to clear it of too many thoughts. "The Reyes family is going to want your brain working for them. They're going to offer you a job soon, I can tell. Just know that you're always welcome here. I'll have a position on my staff ready for you if you ever want it."

"All I want," Nevada admitted, "is to work hard and become your head waiter. Maybe take over managing this store when you expand into a franchise. I like it here, and you've been good to me."

"The Reyes family will be good to you too," Rosto replied, but he smiled. "Don't promise me anything now," he added when Nevada opened his mouth to argue. "See what Reyes offers before you make a decision. Besides, Taylor seems to think he'll be a part of your life from now on. You might want to discuss your future plans with him too."

Nevada couldn't argue with that logic. He also knew he had to tell Rosto the truth about himself. If Rosto couldn't handle the fact that Nevada was a Ge-Mi, then Nevada would have to leave the restaurant anyway.

That was all going to have to be a problem to deal with another day. People were queued up outside the front door, waiting to be let in for their lunch.

"Thanks," Nevada said quickly to Rosto before hurrying to the door to flip the sign to open and unlock it. He held it open so the waiting customers could come inside. With Sing indisposed, Nevada had to take care of the entire restaurant for the lunch rush. It didn't get too busy, but a few tables had to wait longer than Nevada would have liked. Rosto helped deliver trays of food from the kitchen and fill drink orders when he wasn't seating parties. Leslie came in an hour early for her shift and took over all of Nevada's tables so he could get a lunch break.

There was no sign of Carley or Sing for the rest of the day. Taylor also didn't reappear, although Nevada did hear an occasional howl. It brought a smile to his face, a drastic difference from his life just a few weeks ago. His fear of the wolves was gone simply because he had actually spoken to one. Yes, dogs did chase and bite, but not Taylor. At least, Taylor wouldn't chase or bite Nevada with intent to harm.

When Nevada finished his lunch, he and Leslie split the room in half until Ree arrived to take over her portion of the room. The dinner rush hadn't slowed even slightly. Nevada had thought people would get their taste of the new restaurant, and then the lines would slowly die down. That wasn't the case at all. He saw familiar faces and heard stories from parties about how much their friends had recommended they come. The waiting list was an hour long by six thirty, and all Nevada wanted was five minutes off his feet to give them a chance to stop hurting.

The idea that Rosto might turn his little café into a franchise wasn't too farfetched after all, especially given how popular it was. Nevada could practically see Rosto's business wheels turning in his head. At the very least, they needed to think about expanding again to get more tables and a bigger kitchen that could hold multiple sous chefs. Nevada was honestly excited at the prospect.

At the same time, however, he kept waiting for Taylor to come back. Taylor had promised to stay nearby throughout the day, but Nevada hadn't seen him even once.

By seven, the waiting list had shrunk to only forty minutes, and Nevada looked forward to the end of his shift. He was sweaty and tired, and his feet hurt. All of his tables were full, and everyone wanted their food or his attention right away. He didn't even notice when the front door opened to let in more customers until the room quickly quieted.

Nevada half expected to see Taylor or some of his wolves standing in the doorway, but couldn't say he was surprised to see four hyenas standing there instead. He recognized them all from Taylor's house the night before.

"Spread out, keep them in their seats," the female hyena snarled. She didn't move from the doorway and stood stiffly as if she were too injured to do more than give orders. "No phones!" she yelled into the silent room. "I want everyone's hands on the table where I can see them. Anyone who hides their hand loses it. Act like good hostages, and you might get out of here alive tonight."

"We won't make very good hostages," Rosto said sharply from where he was standing in front of the greeting podium.

"Rosto Gregorio," the female hyena said with a bark of high-pitched laughter. "If we hadn't already been ordered to kill you tonight, you would have just signed your death warrant. I hope your blood stains the tiles of the floor so everyone might remember you when you're gone."

One of the male hyenas walked behind Rosto with a threatening grin on his face. Nevada had no doubt he was about to see his boss and good friend die. Where was Taylor when he and his wolves were actually needed? Taylor had promised to keep watch, but Nevada couldn't see any wolves outside the large glass windows. It was up to the people here to fight back, Nevada included.

"We really won't make good hostages," Nevada repeated. He stepped into the middle of the room where he could see all the hyenas.

"You're going to die too!" the female snapped. "I'll kill you myself!"

"I almost tore your spine out last night," Nevada hissed, lifting his upper lip to let his fangs show for perhaps the first time in his entire life. "You think you have a chance against me now?" He was purposefully starting a fight with a Ge-Mi; there was no need to hide what he was any longer. He reached up and pulled the scarf off his head to reveal his ears, ignoring the gasps of shock and dismay that erupted around him.

"It's just you, kitty cat," she sneered. "You have no chance."

Ree let out a high-pitched trill from the left side of the room. One of the hyenas had gotten too close to her. Nevada carefully turned to look without taking his eyes off the leader, hoping he could do something to help Ree. Before he could do anything, Ree punched out with one fist. She hit the hyena right in the throat, sending him crashing to the floor, clutching at his abused windpipe and gasping helplessly for air. She flittered away faster than Nevada's eyes could track her, and a black wig floated to the ground where she had been standing. A riot of colorful feathers covered her head like hair.

"Who said it was just me?" Nevada demanded, although since he hadn't known Ree was also a Ge-Mi, his voice was mostly full of bravado.

Ree let out another trill as she reappeared behind the hyena advancing on Rosto. She kicked him in the back of the knee, sending him sprawling to the ground. Rosto jumped on him, and another man—a regular customer— jumped up from his table to tackle the hyena standing near him.

A brawl erupted as hyena, human, and bird all began fighting. The crash as plates were broken and tables were tossed mixed with screams as others fought to get to safety. Nevada thought he heard Sing's voice calling over the bedlam to direct people out through the kitchen, but he focused on the hyena leader.

Her own bravado had faded once it became clear how outnumbered her small army was. The humans wouldn't last long against the claws and strength of a hyena, but with Ree and Rosto—who knew how to handle Ge-Mis after his time spent with the Reyes—both fighting, Nevada knew the hyenas would lose. Nevada had to stop their leader before she turned tail and made a run for it. She had to know something that would help stop the coup, but she was still close to the door, and no one dared to engage her.

It took Nevada too long to fight through the crowd to get to the door. Although the hyena made it outside, she couldn't run with her injuries, and Nevada didn't have any issues catching up to her. She stood ready for him this time, though, blocking his inexperienced punch with an arm and a bark of laughter. Her nails raked down Nevada's chest, cutting through his uniform shirt like butter and drawing blood. He jumped back and crossed his arms over his body as if he could stop the bleeding with a little pressure.

"You're the reason Ge-Mis like me have to remain in hiding," Nevada snapped. His eyes stung with tears of pain, and he panted in fear. He had never done anything like this before, used to running and hiding for his entire life. Still, he had to keep her here until help arrived, until Taylor arrived. "You enjoy killing and being evil, ruining it for people like me who just want to live a quiet life."

"For people like you?" she scoffed. "You're not a person. You're a Ge-Mi, an abomination of nature like me. We were never meant to exist, so what does it matter if we have a little fun before the laws of nature reassert themselves and we're wiped out of existence?"

Nevada couldn't help taking an involuntary step backward at her horrible words. They couldn't be true; otherwise, why had his mother loved him so much? Why would Taylor's grandfather have kept him if Taylor didn't have a place in this world?

"Where did you hear such a horrible thing like that?" Nevada finally forced out, unwilling to let her words linger in the air. "It's not true."

"She learned it at one of the terrible orphanages set up to house Ge-Mi children," Carley said as he stepped out of the front door of the café. For the first time ever, Carley looked disheveled. His suit was ripped as if claws had gotten caught in the material, and his hair had lost its neat combing. "There aren't any such orphanages in Reyes territory. I'll be able to follow your trail, even if it's all the way back to your orphanage, to get to the root of this. Unless you want to save me the effort by telling me who hired you."

She spat on the ground in answer.

Taylor stepped out of the café behind Carley, and Nevada let out a sigh of relief. He didn't have to fight anymore.

"Give up, hyena," Taylor called as he stepped around Carley and advanced on her. "The rest of your clan has been subdued. Surrender."

She let out a long laugh. "I'd rather die first. Or that you die." She reached under her shirt and pulled out a laser gun. The muzzle pointed toward Taylor, who had frozen in place, shocked.

"You're a Ge-Mi; you've got claws. What do you need a gun for?" he asked, his voice incredulous. Nevada could practically see his brain scrambling for a way to get her to lower the gun.

"I was told to kill you and your supporters. It doesn't matter how I do that, only that I'll be paid well for it." She laughed again, high yipping chuckles that made Nevada's tail twitch restlessly against his knee. She thumbed the power higher on the gun without taking her eyes off Taylor. "Goodbye, Taylor Reyes," she said as her finger tightened on the trigger.

Nevada leapt, fear for Taylor making his jump far more powerful than normal. He let out a chuffing hiss as he slammed into her side. The gun went off with a crack just as Nevada hit her, and Nevada heard Taylor let out a canine yelp of pain.

Nevada didn't have time to focus on Taylor. The hyena was bleeding again, but the gun still rested in her hand. He reached for it, grappling with her even as blood from the scratches on his chest dripped between them to mingle with hers on the pavement. Their hands were both slick with it, and the gun slipped from between Nevada's fingers for one heart-stopping moment before he realized she had also dropped it. They both rolled on the ground trying to get to the gun first, but a shoe kicked it away before either of them could get a hand on it.

"I've got her!" Carley said forcefully. Nevada chanced a look upward and saw Carley holding his own gun, pointing it at the pavement away from them both. Nevada kicked the hyena one last time to create some space between them and then rolled away. Carley snapped up his gun and pointed it at her. She snarled insensibly. Nevada didn't feel light-headed at all, so most of the blood on the ground around the hyena had to be her own. Another glance at Carley showed he still had her in his sights, so Nevada carefully scrambled to his feet and over to where Taylor was slumped on the ground.

For one heart-stopping second, Nevada thought Taylor was dead. Then he heard a pain-filled whine and realized Taylor was in too much pain to move. Nevada dropped to his knees at Taylor's side, but didn't dare touch him.

"Where are you hurt?" Nevada gasped, his own whine apparent in his voice.

"My arm," Taylor bit out. He rolled slightly, and Nevada could see he had one hand clapped over his other arm with blood dripping from his fingers.

"Carley, we need a doctor!" Nevada yelled.

"On his way!" Carley yelled back. Nevada looked over to see him still standing over the hyena where she lay bleeding on the pavement, gun pointed directly at her head. "Find something to wrap it with."

Nevada's shirt was already in tatters; he took one of the cleaner-looking shreds and ripped it the rest of the way off his body before carefully pushing Taylor's hand away to wrap a makeshift bandage around Taylor's arm. Nevada pressed his own hands against the wound to help staunch the blood.

"You're hurt too," Taylor whispered. His free, blood-covered hand reached out to touch one of the scratches gently.

Nevada let out a hiss of pain but didn't pull away. "It'll heal with a good lick or three," he replied. "You're the one who needs help."

"Yeah, probably. Thank you for jumping to save me." Taylor's eyes slid closed as he slurred his last words.

"Taylor! Stay awake!" Nevada yelled, shaking him slightly, but Taylor's eyes didn't open again. He was still breathing, but that didn't reassure Nevada at all.

Five cars dropped from the air and screeched to a stop in the street without bothering to engage their hydraulics to land properly. The owl from the day before—Oliver, if Nevada remembered his name correctly—bolted out of the car first, and he ran to Taylor's side.

"I'm going to need a stretcher and an IV," he called over his shoulder. His eyesight must've been good enough to see Taylor's injuries from so far away. The hatchback on one of the cars opened, and three men came hurrying after Oliver toward Taylor. "Let go," Oliver said gently to Nevada when he reached Taylor's side. Oliver's rough grip on Nevada's clenched fingers forced Nevada to let go before his words could register.

"He got shot," Nevada tried to explain, but his words were full of too much air to make much sense. The world spun gently around him.

"Get me another stretcher!" Oliver yelled. After a few moments, a second stretcher appeared through the throng of people who had poured out of the cars after Oliver. They all wore the bluish metal armor of Lord Reyes's troops and carried guns far larger than Carley's. Nevada saw three of them head toward Carley, and the rest split between securing the street and heading into the café.

Nevada blinked, and when he opened his eyes again, he found himself lying on the stretcher. A woman with a mouth much too wide for her face filled with sharply pointed teeth inspected his chest while Oliver continued to give instructions about laser paste and shock blankets from nearby.

"You'll be just fine," the woman told him with a wide smile that didn't reassure him the least bit. "You'll go to sleep now, and when you wake up, we'll have you all stitched up. Don't you worry."

"Wha' 'bout Taylor?" Nevada slurred, his tongue feeling thick and heavy in his mouth even as his eyes slid involuntarily shut again.

"He's in safe hands too. We'll do what we can for him; never fear. Now sleep."

Nevada didn't mean to obey her, but he didn't have a choice. Though he fought it, the world faded away, and he knew nothing more.

Chapter Seven

Everything was too bright, even through his closed eyelids. Nevada groaned and tried to lift his arm to cover his eyes, but heavy blankets weighed it down. He fought with them for a few ineffectual moments before realizing he would have to open his eyes and actually see where his arm was tangled in order to get it free. It was still too bright for that, though, so Nevada let out another unhappy groan.

"We've got a live one!" someone chirped happily, far too close to Nevada, and he jumped in surprise. "What do you need?" she asked, still sounding far too perky.

"Bright," Nevada mumbled through lips that felt heavy and difficult to move. "No light."

"Right-o," she chirped again. Nevada heard a rustling sound as she moved, and then the room darkened abruptly.

Nevada slowly opened his eyes, blinking to try to focus them in the dim room. He didn't recognize where he was, but then the off-white ceiling he could see from his prone position could belong anywhere.

A woman with a riot of colorful feathers for hair leaned over the bed so Nevada could see her. She looked eerily like Ree, though she was definitely older.

"You're not Ree," Nevada forced out, hoping to get some answers as to where he was and why.

"Nope. I'm Leigh. I hatched Ree myself though. Good kid, even if she likes wearing those silly wigs of hers." The woman grinned, still leaning over Nevada, but her eyes studied his face closely as if she was looking for something.

"I think it's time to lower your pain meds a little more," she said, finally stepping out of Nevada's sight. "Your chest might hurt a bit, but we got those scratches all cleaned up, and you're healing nicely. Might not even scar with the false skin stitches the doc decided to use. Now, your friend the wolf: he had to get laser stitches. Only way to heal a gunshot wound like his is to cut out the burned skin first and then start patching him together. Even with the false skin, he'll still scar." She tsked unhappily from wherever she was working.

Nevada didn't know if it was the lowering of the pain meds or Leigh's sharp reminder, but the memory of the last time Nevada had seen Taylor blasted through him like a spark. He struggled to sit up, but the blankets were still too heavy.

"Whoops, here you go," Leigh chirped. She hit some sort of switch, and the bed began to fold up until Nevada was in a sitting position.

"Taylor's going to be okay?" Nevada asked before he was even up all the way.

"That scraggly wolf? He's been shot worse, trust me. Was up and about an hour ago, demanding to see you and wanting to know what was so wrong that you hadn't woken up yet." Leigh smiled fondly as she spoke. "Those hyena claws that got you were none too clean, so we had to fight off a nasty infection, but now you're right as rain. Should I tell the wolf that you're up, or do you want to wait until the pain meds fade a bit more so you're actually coherent?"

Nevada wanted to see Taylor was okay with his own eyes rather than accept Leigh's assurances. "I want to see Taylor," Nevada confirmed.

"Right-o," Leigh chirped. She hurried into the hallway and vanished around a corner.

Nevada surveyed the plain, utilitarian room. The off-white walls matched the ceiling and held no adornment. A thick gray blanket rested on top of the white sheets on his bed. A metal tower sat to his left, where Leigh had been working. There was a touchscreen at the top that appeared to run the machine. A single thin, opaque tube led from the tower to Nevada's arm, where it snaked under the blankets and disappeared.

Loud footsteps sounded in the hallway outside, and Nevada looked up just in time to see Taylor rush into the room. His anxious smile reached his eyes, bright and eager. His tail wagged, too, but Nevada immediately focused on the thick bandage wrapped around his right bicep.

"Are you okay?" Nevada asked.

Taylor glanced down at his arm and shrugged. "The blast took out some muscle, but it missed the bone. A bit of physical therapy and I'll be just fine. How are you?" He hovered at Nevada's bedside, and though his tail continued to wag, his hands were in the air as if he didn't dare touch anything.

"I think the doctor was just being overcautious," Nevada explained, trying to parse through everything Leigh had chirped at him.

"Aren't they always," Taylor said with a groan and an exasperated roll of his eyes. "Don't jump on this. Don't climb on that. Honestly, it's just a gunshot wound."

Nevada laughed, and Taylor grinned with him. Taylor's good hand reached out slowly toward Nevada, and Nevada ducked his head so Taylor could touch his ear.

"You're so fluffy," Taylor sighed, gently rubbing his fingers along the arch of Nevada's ear.

"And you're both high on pain meds," Leigh agreed as she stepped into the room, looking cross. A man behind her pushed an empty wheelchair. "Sit down before you fall down, idiot."

Taylor sat on the side of Nevada's bed, his hand not moving from Nevada's ear. "Here's good, right? Next to my fluffy kitty cat. I like my fluffy kitty cat."

"That should be my cue to leave, I suppose," Carley said from the doorway, stuck behind the man with the wheelchair.

Taylor let out a heavy sigh. After two tries and Leigh eventually coming over to help, he swung his legs all the way up onto the bed. He leaned back against the raised headboard next to Nevada and turned to look at Carley.

"What's up, Carley-barley?" Taylor asked with another wide grin.

"He's clearly high as a kite. You'll probably want to talk to him later," Leigh noted.

"If only I could," Carley said. He stepped around the wheelchair and strode up to the bed. "You will be happy to know, Nevada, that I went to feed your half-dozen cats. I filled all their food and water bowls, but they remained in hiding the entire time. Except for this one." He reached into the breast pocket of his suit and carefully pulled out Hex. Hex mewed pointedly at Nevada, who couldn't help but laugh. "He latched onto me and refused to let go. I figured he wanted to see you, so I brought him and took some supplies from your home. I hope you don't mind."

Nevada tried to lift his arms, but was stymied by the blanket again. He struggled with it for a moment, and Taylor turned to try to help pull the blanket down with his good arm, but Nevada didn't get free until Leigh, exasperated, came to help. Carley deposited Hex into Nevada's hands and then stepped back.

Hex purred happily, circling around Nevada's cupped palms and sniffing his fingers. He jumped from there onto Taylor's lap, where he curled up for naptime. Taylor immediately began to stroke Hex with the hand of his good arm, and Carley lifted an eyebrow in surprise.

"Not going to try killing this one?" Carley asked.

"I think Hex would gut me if I tried," Taylor admitted drunkenly. "He's vicious. I like him. Can we keep him?"

"If your grandfather says it's okay," Carley replied with practiced ease.

The drugs must've been easing from Nevada's system because his brain was working much better now; or Taylor's warmth pressed against his side and the jolt of adrenaline it caused helped clear his head. Still, he needed to know what had happened after Taylor had been shot.

"How's the café? And Rosto?" Nevada asked.

"Both a little banged up, but not too bad," Carley replied. "The restaurant was closed today and will probably be closed tomorrow, but that's mostly because the majority of the waitstaff is unable to work. You and Ree are in the hospital—she's fine," Carley quickly added when Nevada jumped in alarm. "Sing is still spilling his life story and will not be allowed to return to work until after I've completely cleared him, if at all. Rosto and Leslie are both sporting some decent bruises but are otherwise okay. Together, they're getting new tables, chairs, and dishes to replace what was broken. The café and restaurant should both reopen by the end of the week, right in time for the grand opening."

Though he was glad to hear it, Nevada didn't know if Rosto would allow him back. The tight feeling in Nevada's chest told him that Rosto probably wouldn't. Nevada had lied to Rosto about what he was for years, and anyway, what shop manager would want a Ge-Mi for an employee?

To distract himself, he changed the subject. "What about the hyenas?"

Carley's grin turned predatory. "Their leader didn't make it; she bled out before we could stabilize her. Luckily, I got enough information beforehand to start tracking her, and the rest of her clan has been talking. We should be able to finish tracking her movements before she arrived here and figure out who hired her."

Nevada knew he ought to feel bad about the hyena's death. His clawing up her back combined with his fight over her gun had exacerbated those wounds and was no doubt what killed her. But Nevada was glad she was dead. He never wanted to see someone point a gun at anyone he loved again and would have leapt at her a second time if it kept Taylor safe.

"I tracked her down to an orphanage in the Kingdom of Miami where she was named Spot. Considering the conditions, it's no surprise she left as soon as she could escape and traveled around to dozens of cities, picking up other abandoned hyenas as she went. She lived in Morse for three years before abruptly uprooting her clan and coming here. I only need to identify who traveled to Morse to hire her within that specific timeframe." Carley smiled excitedly at the prospect.

Taylor's head thumped gently down on top of Nevada's, and a soft snore came out of his mouth as his cheek slid down to rest on Nevada's shoulder.

"Finally," Leigh whispered. "Those drugs should have had him out hours ago. Let's get him back to his own bed before he wakes again."

"Couldn't you just bring him an extra blanket?" Nevada asked. He carefully tilted his head to look at Taylor and couldn't help but smile at Taylor's sleeping face.

Something flashed briefly, and Nevada looked over at Carley to see him putting his phone back in his pocket. Carley grinned conspiratorially at him.

"Just a picture to show Lord Reyes that Taylor is recovering well. I'm sure the hospital staff would be happy to bring another blanket instead of chancing that moving Taylor will wake him up. I'll stop by again tomorrow." He nodded politely to Nevada and Leigh before turning on his heel and walking out of the room.

"Fine," Leigh grumped. She walked over to the tower and hit a button on the touchscreen that made the bed slowly flatten out again. "I'll bring a blanket, but you had both better nap for the rest of the day."

Nevada had to admit a nap sounded nice. Taylor's warmth and Hex's soft purring surrounded him comfortably. Leigh brought over another blanket and carefully spread it over Taylor and Nevada's freed arms. Nevada let out a yawn and snuggled his nose into Taylor's shoulder where he could breathe in Taylor's scent despite its astringent, hospital tinge. He closed his eyes and quickly fell asleep.

*

When Nevada told Taylor he was being released from the hospital after just two days, Nevada could immediately see how annoyed Taylor was in the way he huffed angrily at Nevada's words; Taylor still had at least three more days before the doctors would consider discharging him despite all his whining and grumbling, and Nevada knew staying there when Nevada had already been released must feel agonizing. The pout and low growl Taylor let out when Nevada came to say goodbye was evidence enough of that, despite Nevada promising he would come visit every day.

After finally forcing himself to leave Taylor to the safe hands of the doctors, Nevada went to his apartment where he contended with his miffed cats. Only Maya came up to him, and she was more interested in where Hex had ended up than saying hello to Nevada.

"Taylor has him," Nevada explained. "Princess Pea will probably end up looking after him when Taylor goes home."

Maya let out an unhappy *mrr* and then stalked off.

Nevada sighed, unsurprised by the cold welcome, and went to get an apology out of the treat drawer. On top of their full food bowls—which was probably the best indication his cats were pissed since they really liked to eat—he put a few treats he kept for special occasions. Then he went to shower.

By the time he had finally gotten the hospital smell out of his fur, the bowls were empty. Beth waited for him outside the bathroom, and he knelt to give her a good scratch under the chin while she meowed at him to tell him she was happy he had returned.

"I have to go out again, but I'll be back tonight," he promised. Beth took a few moments to decide if that was acceptable before meowing her approval. She headed to her favorite scratching post, and Nevada jumped for his loft.

His hairbrush lay right where it had been dropped the other night, still full of red and white fur. Nevada smiled at it for a bit before cleaning it and quickly brushing out his tail. He put on his usual pants and a random T-shirt, but he left off a headscarf. Everyone already knew his secret, and Lord Reyes had no intention of throwing him out of the city. Nevada needed to know if Rosto felt the same.

Nevada couldn't help stalling by running the brush through the hair on his head, careful of his ears, but he knew that waiting to learn what Rosto had to say was only prolonging the agony. Nevada firmly put the brush down and jumped from the loft. He gathered his keys, said goodbye to his cats, and left.

The short walk to the restaurant felt longer than usual. People stared at him this time, not at Taylor standing next to him. He could see the fear in their eyes, but he also saw recognition. He had lived peacefully among them as a human for three years; the only difference between a week ago and today was that his ears were throwing off some of his neighbors. He was the one who had helped them adopt a kitten, smiled at them politely every morning, or served them lunch at the café every day for three years, and his interactions with them tempered their automatic disgust at seeing a Ge-Mi. It would take time for the community to decide how to treat him.

When Nevada arrived at the café, he found the door already unlocked and the sign turned to OPEN. He went inside and saw the shelves fully stocked with baked goods. The restaurant half of the building was dark and quiet, though the lunch rush had ended long ago. There were only a few customers left in the café. Rosto and Leslie were working, but when they caught sight of him, they both quickly finished their tasks and came over to him.

"You're okay!" Leslie gasped. "I couldn't get any information out of anyone, aside from Rosto here telling me you were in the hospital. How are you feeling?"

"I've healed," Nevada replied, relieved that Leslie didn't seem to care in the least about his ears.

"You have a tail too?" Rosto asked sharply, cutting off anything further Leslie had been about to ask.

"I do, but none of my pants have holes in them for it. Taylor said he'll have some special made for me," Nevada explained.

"So you're done hiding who you are then?" Rosto continued.

"There's no point in hiding when everyone already knows," Nevada admitted cautiously. "Even if you hate me, I still have Taylor. I'll find somewhere else to work if I have to."

"Carley will still hire you," Rosto said pointedly, and Nevada's heart sank. Rosto, the first person to ever care for him after his mother's death, would fire him because he was a Ge-Mi.

"Only if I don't have a job here any longer," Nevada said, trying not to put too much hope into his words.

"You still want to work here?" Rosto asked, his voice full of curiosity. Nevada looked up at him for the first time since walking in the door, but Rosto's face was blank.

"Yes, but only if you'll let me," Nevada said.

"Let you? Nevada, I just bought another property on the other side of town. I'm starting a franchise, and I want you to stay here as assistant manager while Leslie and I get the other store organized."

"Assistant manager?" Nevada said, gaping at Rosto, desperately hoping this wasn't some kind of joke.

"You asked for the position, and I know you deserve it. Who cares if you're part cat? You do a good job, and that's all that matters to me." Rosto was smiling as he spoke, but Nevada was trying to hold in tears.

"I'm a snow leopard," he said out loud for the first time in his life.

"Your tail must be so pretty," Leslie said.

Before Nevada could think of a response, Rosto's cell phone rang. He pulled it out of his pocket and looked at the caller ID on the screen; then he frowned and immediately answered it.

"He's what?" Rosto exclaimed after a brief moment of listening to the voice at the other end. "Well, Nevada's here. Let me ask him." Rosto pulled the phone away from his mouth for a moment and turned toward Nevada. "Taylor's gone; checked himself out of the hospital. He hasn't gone to his grandfather's place or his pack's den. Do you know where he might go?"

Nevada looked out the window to the street, half expecting to see Taylor walking toward him right then. "He might have gone to my apartment," he said. "I can go check."

"Good idea," Rosto agreed. "You have my number, right? Call when you get there."

"I will." Nevada headed back to the door, hoping he'd find Taylor safe. Taylor was too injured to be wandering around the city alone, especially when they still didn't know who had hired the hyenas.

"Nevada, we're reopening the restaurant this weekend for our big opening night. I'll need you here," Rosto called as Nevada's hand touched the door handle.

Nevada looked over his shoulder and grinned at Rosto and Leslie. "I'll be there." He hurried out the door and retraced his steps to his apartment.

He could easily discern Taylor's smell right in front of the building, even when it was tinged with astringent notes from the hospital. It was fresh, which meant he had been here recently. Nevada quickly unlocked the front door and hurried up the stairs, glad to be following Taylor's scent. He stepped into his apartment and saw Maya scolding Hex. The kitten held his ground stubbornly, meowing fiercely at her. Nevada ignored them, looking around the apartment to find Taylor.

The bathroom door stood wide open, and Taylor couldn't hide behind all the cat paraphernalia under the loft, which only meant one thing.

"You had better have showered before you climbed into my bed," Nevada called upward.

Taylor groaned in the loft. "It was hard enough just getting up here. By the time the pain meds wore off and I remembered, I was too sore and tired to get down again."

Nevada let out a heavy sigh. "You're going to have to pay to get all my blankets and pillows washed, and if the hospital smell doesn't come out, you're replacing them."

"Deal," Taylor replied immediately.

Nevada sighed again, but didn't argue anymore. Instead, he headed over to the phone built into the wall. He couldn't afford a cell phone on the money he made working at the café, but as assistant manager that might change. Luckily, most homes, including his, came with a built-in phone attached to the security system, so Nevada used that to call Rosto.

"He's here," Nevada said once the phone connected. "He's stuck in my loft and won't be going anywhere anytime soon. Tell the doctor to send his medication here."

"How'd he get stuck in your loft?" Rosto asked with a laugh.

"Because he's an idiot," Nevada replied fondly.

"Thanks for finding him," Rosto said once he finished laughing. "I'll pass the message along." He hung up, and Nevada turned to look at the loft. Even though he didn't need the extra momentum, he took a running leap and landed lightly up in the loft.

"Hello," Nevada said. He had landed on the edge, unsure where Taylor was and unwilling to bump him and exacerbate his injury. Nevada crawled closer to where Taylor lay on top of all the blankets and pillows. He smelled like the hospital, but underneath Nevada detected his familiar scent.

"Hello," Taylor replied with a strained smile. "My pain meds wore off."

Nevada shrugged. "I'm sure someone will be by soon to give you some. Rosto's letting everyone know where you are."

"That's good. I guess. More meds would be nice, but I couldn't stay at that hospital when you weren't there anymore."

That was sweet to hear, but it was also stupid. "You're not healed yet," Nevada scolded, frowning at Taylor.

"It's just a gunshot wound; a little pain until it's healed and some rehabilitation for the arm."

"You shouldn't have been walking around the city unprotected when whoever's trying to kill you is still at large," Nevada added, still upset.

Taylor shook his head. "Yeah, that was probably stupid, but I wasn't exactly thinking clearly. I wanted to be with you, so I headed here. I'm glad to see you."

"I'm glad too," Nevada admitted easily. "Nap until the doctor arrives with more medicine."

"Probably should," Taylor agreed. He patted the pillows next to him with his good arm. "Come nap with me."

Nevada couldn't resist. He kicked his shoes off and tossed them over the edge of the loft in the general direction of the door, hoping he didn't hit any cats, and carefully pulled the blankets out from under Taylor. Then, Nevada climbed into bed and pulled the blankets up to cover them both.

Taylor lifted his hand gently, running his fingers over Nevada's ears. He let out a contented sigh. Nevada purred slightly at the touch and curled closer to Taylor. Despite his pain, it didn't take Taylor long to fall asleep. Nevada lay beside him feeling safe, content, loved, and warm under the blankets.

Nevada still worried about the grand opening of the restaurant, the person trying to create a coup, his Ge-Mi status now he'd outed himself, and finding time for everyone to heal properly before the next fight. After a moment, he decided to forget about it all for a while and enjoy what he had right then. He snuggled even tighter against Taylor, careful of the wounded arm, and let Taylor's warm presence soothe him into sleep.

Ge-Mi

Part Two

Prologue

Taylor Reyes knew the exact moment he fell in love. He had been ranting and raving and basically making an ass of himself. Okay, if he really thought about it, Taylor knew a lot of people would say he did that regularly, but this time was different. A baby kitten had attacked him earlier in the day. The scabs on his face were itching, and his pride was smarting. The first chance he got, he tracked the cat stench that belonged to some waiter at a restaurant where his grandfather insisted he eat. The waiter's cat was the one that attacked him, and Taylor wasn't about to let the waiter go unpunished for the slight. The stench led down the sidewalk a few blocks to a nearby apartment building, and eventually, to the tiny studio apartment taking up a third of the top floor.

Getting inside was easy enough since his DNA had been automatically coded into every lock in the entire city. It was one of the perks of being the heir to the Reyes family, the family that had ruled the city of Kensey for generations. Kensey Reyes had taken power directly after the last Great War that destroyed all the large cities, leaving behind only smaller cities and towns without any federal government to oversee them. Those with the means took control all across the country, and Kensey held on to his city fiercely until his death ten years later. Taylor's great-grandfather and then eventually his grandfather had taken power, and Taylor was being groomed as the next heir.

Taylor enjoyed a life of privilege, but as a Ge-Mi, it wasn't an easy life to live. Long before the Great War, scientists had managed to combine the DNA of humans with that of animals. Today's history books contained speculation on why the scientists had done that, but it was generally believed the project began with good intentions. A cure for blindness by giving someone the sight ability of an eagle was the example Taylor remembered from his school textbook. Unfortunately, the military and some unsavory groups became involved, and they wanted super speed or super strength. Strange hybrid creatures were the eventual result, people like Taylor, who appeared human enough but also had wolf ears and a tail, or people with the power of a bear or the venom of a snake.

At first, Ge-Mis and humans had been able to live together peacefully, but fear over a Ge-Mi's extra abilities soon had the humans enacting discriminatory laws that forced even the most law-abiding Ge-Mis into desperate acts to keep their families fed.

After the Great War, that fear remained, coloring the minds of all the humans in the country. No one really remembered why the Great War started, but it had increased the level of fear regular people experienced.

That fear now focused on the Ge-Mis. It wasn't easy to be called the heir of the city when almost no one trusted that his animal half would be safe in the position of the city's next leader.

Taylor's father was a red wolf Ge-Mi, and he had passed down the red-colored, pointed wolf ears that sat on top of Taylor's head as well as a long and fluffy red wolf's tail. The rest of him was pure Reyes stock—light-blond hair and blue eyes—but the Ge-Mi parts of him were too distinct to hide.

Which was totally unlike the object of Taylor's affection.

He had expected to find a human hoarder of cats, and he found a hoarder, but Nevada most definitely wasn't human. The moment those big gray eyes with the adorable little rounded ears peeking out of his white-and-black hair appeared over the edge of the loft high above Taylor, his heart was lost.

Nevada was no pushover. He wasn't some kitty cat Taylor could threaten into obedience or scare away by growling. No, Nevada was all snow leopard, fierce and protective of those he loved. Yet, at the same time, it was easy for him to hide his small ears under a handkerchief and to keep his tail wrapped around one leg. He had been hiding among the humans for his entire life.

Taylor had discovered Nevada's secret that fateful night, but where he might have ordinarily used it to blackmail Nevada, he was unable to do it. Nevada was just so... Taylor didn't have the words to describe the way

Nevada made him feel, but Nevada owned his heart all the same.

Which was why Taylor was currently standing across the street from Restaurant Spice, hidden in a darkened alcove where he couldn't be seen, watching as Nevada deftly moved through the tables stuffed with customers.

These days, Nevada didn't have to hide what he was. He'd spent three years working at the café next door while hiding his Ge-Mi side, and the customers genuinely learned to like him. Recent events in a fight against a clan of hyena Ge-Mis trying to kill him forced Nevada to reveal his snow leopard half. The handkerchief was gone now, his ears visible to the world, and because Taylor had arranged to have special pants made for Nevada with an elastic ring in the back for his tail, his tail now showed. However, he still kept it curled around one leg, half out of habit and half to keep the kids from tugging on it when they saw it because the white fur with black rosettes was distinctive inside the busy restaurant.

Taylor pulled his phone from his pocket to double-check the time and sighed. It was only 7:45 p.m., which meant he had at least fifteen more minutes before Nevada got off shift. It would probably be longer, though, since Nevada was slowly starting to learn the ropes of the assistant manager position and didn't leave until he was certain the restaurant could run without him there.

Ree's riot of multicolored feathers, where her hair would have been had she been human, appeared in front of a table in the window, temporarily blocking Taylor's view. Ree was another Ge-Mi who had been outed in the hyena attack, but she, too, seemed to be thriving as another waiter at the restaurant.

Taylor let out a low growl and slumped harder against the wall behind him. Waiting for Nevada was so damned difficult, but the last time he went into the restaurant to get Nevada, he had been scolded for bothering the customers during dinner. A mad Nevada wasn't a fun Nevada.

Taylor's phone rang, startling him into jumping slightly in surprise. A glance at the caller ID told him Carley was calling.

"What?" Taylor growled into the phone. Carley knew Taylor was waiting to walk Nevada home. After closing was the only guaranteed time they had together each day, considering how busy both Taylor and Nevada were at their respective jobs.

"I might have found the link we need to finally find out who's engineering the coup," Carley explained, completely unperturbed by Taylor's aggressive tone. Carley had changed Taylor's diapers; he wasn't afraid of any of Taylor's moods.

"Who?" Taylor asked, all growl gone from his voice.

"Not sure yet," Carley replied, and Taylor could hear a cheeky shrug in Carley's voice. The man loved to yank Taylor's tail. "But I know where to start digging. Get your kitty cat home safe; then come over."

"Fine." Taylor let out a grumbling sigh to let Carley know how dissatisfied he was before hanging up.

Chapter One

Hunts through the city that didn't go well were probably the most frustrating thing in Taylor's life. His pack had caught the scent of the cousin Carley was certain had a hand in the coup and tracked it down, only to lose it in a parking lot. Antony Reyes had gotten into a car and flown off, and that was something even Taylor with his excellent nose couldn't follow.

It was up to Carley to pick up the trail now, Taylor knew, but it still burned inside to have come so close and failed. That was his wolf half talking, of course. Grandpa had been very stern with Taylor growing up—he had to be, given how wild Taylor had been—and Taylor could now tell what parts of him were animal instinct and what parts of him were human. That those parts often overlapped to the point that they were interchangeable was something Taylor had never quite been able to explain to Gramps and Carley.

What really sucked about the failed hunt was that it had lasted until well after dawn. The apartment to which Taylor was heading would already be empty, but he needed the comfort, so he was going there anyway.

The DNA scanner at the door let him in quickly, and Taylor hurried up the three flights of stairs to Nevada's apartment door, which he opened with a real key this time. Nevada had given him the key, Taylor remembered as his tail wagged happily behind him. Now he didn't need his lockpicks anymore. The door opened to a chorus of meows, half of which turned into disgusted snarls when they saw it was him again.

"Yeah, yeah. Ankle biters," Taylor said to the cats with a sneer that lifted enough of his upper lip to show a bit of fang. He wasn't afraid of the brood of cats Nevada kept on hand. They could be plenty menacing, but he was a wolf so they were no match for him. He was afraid of Nevada though, which was why he headed straight to the bathroom instead of to bed like he would have if he had gone back to the pack house.

Nevada wasn't a neat freak, but he liked things clean. A good way to piss him off was to curl up in his nest of pillows and blankets without having showered recently. Taylor liked marking his scent all over Nevada's apartment—and he was thankfully human enough not to need to pee everywhere. Nevada understood that urge since cats had it too, but to him there was a big difference between a clean and a dirty scent. Taylor got in the shower with a huff and started scrubbing.

Relationships meant sacrifices, Gramps had explained, the one time Taylor had whined to him about having to pay to get Nevada's bed dry-cleaned—again. Having to take an extra ten minutes to shower before bed wasn't really a sacrifice at all, and Nevada's happiness whenever he noticed Taylor doing that made the effort worth it, but it rankled all the same.

The sacrifice was in changing his long-ingrained habits for the happiness of someone else. It took effort, but it was effort he saw returned whenever he opened the fridge and found steak there instead of fish, because Nevada knew that while Taylor liked fish fine, red meat was what made him happiest. Nevada had changed his shopping habits for Taylor, among other things, so Taylor could suck it up and shower.

He finished in the bathroom quickly and took a few extra minutes to brush out his tail so it wouldn't mat, then went back into the main room.

No cats greeted him this time, which meant Nevada must have taken Hex to work with him again, but Taylor could hear rustling noises that said he was being watched. He climbed the ladder that was now always hanging down from the loft where Nevada kept his sleeping area and went over to a set of drawers where he kept some clothes. Taylor pulled on a pair of boxers, carefully fitting his tail through the elastic hole in the back, and fell into bed.

The scents on the pillows and blankets were perfect. He could smell himself and he could smell Nevada's particular scent of cat and food from the restaurant. Those scents melded together, soothing Taylor's frayed emotions. He curled up underneath a thick quilt and drifted off to sleep.

*

The blaring ring of his phone woke Taylor. He grumbled something incoherent, even to himself, as one hand slipped out from under the warmth of the blankets to pat the spot where he usually left his phone. It was empty, and it took his tired brain an extra few seconds to realize the ringing was coming from below. Taylor had left his phone in his pants pocket, which was downstairs where his pants lay in a pile on the bathroom floor. The last thing Taylor wanted to do at the moment was get up, but as the ringing died off and then a few seconds later started again, Taylor slowly pushed the blankets off and crawled out of bed.

The ladder was rope and wooden slats, and it wasn't a good idea to climb down while only half-awake. Taylor landed on the floor with a hard thump after missing a step halfway down. One of the cats let out a startled yowl, to which Taylor growled back. The phone went silent, but started ringing again a second later.

Taylor finally found his discarded pants and the pocket the phone was in.

"Hello?" Taylor growled into the phone.

"We found Antony." Carley's voice was sharp and to the point, but Taylor also thought there was a touch of unhappiness mixed into those three short words. The tone was enough for Taylor to know the news wasn't good.

"What happened?" Taylor started pulling on his pants and cast around for his missing shirt.

Carley took a long moment to answer, which was an answer in itself. "Looks like someone pushed him from a car. He fell a few hundred feet to a, thankfully, empty parking lot below."

Which meant Antony was now a bloody pancake. Taylor didn't know how he felt about that. He had grown up with Antony, who was only two years older than Taylor. As kids, Antony hadn't cared that Taylor had ears, a tail, and a tendency to nip. That had changed when they grew into teenagers, and somewhere, for some reason, Antony learned to hate and fear Ge-Mis as a whole, and Taylor in particular. That was why Taylor wasn't surprised to learn Antony was involved with the scheme to unseat their grandfather. But it was surprising to learn someone had most likely killed Antony.

"My guess is someone found out we were looking to speak with Antony, but Antony knew too much so they had to silence him," Carley said in an echo of Taylor's thoughts. "Hopefully, that means it's someone close to Antony, and we can find them quickly. Anyway, can you get down here with your pack and sniff around, see if you recognize any smells on the body?" He gave Taylor an address on the other side of town, which was really only two miles from Nevada's apartment since the city wasn't exactly huge.

Taylor had no interest in seeing the mangled remains of his cousin, but he did want to know if the scent of whoever pushed Antony out of the car had lingered. "I'll give the pack a call, and we'll be over in about twenty minutes."

It took twenty-five minutes to round everyone up and get across town. He met the pack at their house, a two-story home at the foot of the hill—on top of which the Kensey mansion had been built—with a very large, fenced-in yard that they could all run around in. They took off through the city at a jog.

Taylor was in front, leading the charge as the pack alpha. Drew and LeeAnne were right behind him. Drew was a gray wolf from nose to tail, with overgrown gray hair that hid his ears and a whipcord-thin gray tail. He hadn't grown up in the city, but instead, in a wolf pack that had taken over a bit of unclaimed wild area that separated the cities and towns. He left when he was old enough for that alpha to feel challenged by another strong male in the pack and ended up in Kensey with Taylor, but the wildness from his childhood was evident in almost everything he did.

LeeAnne was the opposite. She looked more wolflike with brown-and-black hair, yellow eyes, and a dark birthmark on her nose, but she was the one who made them all sweep the house every once in a while. LeeAnne might not have grown up in a mansion like Taylor had, but she knew how to play by society's rules in a way Drew and even Taylor never would. They both brought equally important strengths to the pack, and that was why Taylor had them at his back. The rest of the pack—another six wolves—fell in behind.

They weren't stopped as they ran through the city. No one tried to hit them with a car or even honked at them. Taylor remembered when he had first started forming the pack and running around like this was dangerous. It wasn't possible to tell if people were more afraid of retribution for harming Taylor, afraid of getting hounded by the wolves, or whether they had grown more accepting of the Ge-Mis, but it was nice not to have to watch over his shoulder for a car darting down from the sky highway overhead or shooting out from a nearby parking lot.

Carley and Oliver were waiting for the pack when they finally reached the parking lot in question. The lot itself was empty of cars. They were in an area of the city that was almost entirely comprised of shops, which meant it had been empty late at night when Antony fell into it. Carley had two guards standing by the entrance to the lot, just to the side of where cars would descend to park, and their bluish metal armor and laser guns holstered at their hips were keeping the onlookers and any potential parkers away.

Taylor tilted his head to one side and then the other and heard the soft pads of footsteps as his pack peeled off to either side to start investigating. He continued onward to Carley. The lot was a mess. It reeked of blood and bone and decay, for one, which had Taylor scrunching up his nose in disgust. He liked the smell of raw and bleeding meat, but this meat had been out in the sun for a little bit too long for his taste. It looked like the body had mostly gone splat in place. The head was oddly flattened on one side and slightly gooey looking, but it was still attached to the torso, which had split open to spill intestines onto the pavement.

Carley was wearing his usual three-piece suit, looking as neat and pressed as always, even surrounded by body parts. He immediately turned toward Taylor as Taylor reached his side.

"What do you think?" he asked. His voice was devoid of any emotion, as was his face, but this wasn't the first murder scene he had overseen, nor would it likely be his last.

Taylor eyed the way the body had split so evenly down the torso and took another sniff of the air. He snorted to clear the scent out a second later.

"Has the body been lying there long enough to start rotting?" he asked Carley.

Oliver was the one who answered. "Time of death is at least twelve hours ago, but I'd put it closer to eighteen or twenty. I can't say for certain until I take a look at the decomposition level in a microscope."

He was a barn owl Ge-Mi, and his hooked nose, wide-spaced eyes, and brown feathers instead of hair made it very difficult to hide what he was. He was also a very accomplished doctor, which was almost unheard of in the Ge-Mi world. Oliver had been lucky. The mascot of the college where he had applied had been an owl, and the dean had a sick sense of humor. Taylor doubted they had expected Oliver to excel, but he had graduated with full honors. He was wearing jeans and a scrub shirt and started taking off a pair of green latex gloves as he turned toward Taylor and Carley.

"As far as I've been able to tell, the body has only been in this parking lot for four to six hours." Carley frowned down at the oddly flattened head.

"I'd say he was gutted," Taylor added with another look at that far too even split in the torso, "and then tossed out of a car to try to hide the evidence."

"Then we're searching for someone capable of looking a man in the eye when they kill him," Carley said. He shook his head, and the first expression of disgust Taylor had seen at the scene crossed his face. "A real murderer."

"Possibly a serial murderer." Oliver's voice was matter-of-fact, and he crossed his arms over his chest as if he needed to huddle in on himself for just having the thought. "A cut that even and the precision of the drop into the parking lot...?" He trailed off contemplatively.

"We haven't had enough murders in this city to call anything a serial killing," Carley said in sharp disagreement. "And there hasn't been a single other body dumped like this."

He would know since Gramps had put him in charge of security for the city. Carley kept track of everything, from the guards that secured the Kensey mansion, to the city patrols that ensured crime was at a minimum. The patrols included Taylor's pack. It was a job Carley took extremely seriously.

"What if he's not from this city?" Taylor asked out loud as the thought came to him. "It could be another import like the hyenas were."

Carley nodded slowly. "That's a good thought, Taylor. I'll get a team started on researching serial murders or assassins for hire known to be working in other cities. See if we might be able to narrow down who it might be." He paused, once again looking down at the mangled body for a long moment, before continuing. "I'm also going to increase covert patrols throughout the city. If I do anything overt, the populace will start getting nervous, which will only hurt the Reyes's reputation. Expect to see unfamiliar faces patrolling around the pack house and your Nevada's apartment, but be wary since you won't know who is working for me and who might be the killer."

A good point, which made Taylor frown. The stench of rot was starting to make his head swim, but he could still tell it would be dangerous not to know who was creeping around behind his back.

"Make them wear a special lapel pin or an earring or something; that way I can identify them as ours without needing to confront them about it," he finally said.

Carley nodded to show his agreement, but before he could open his mouth to say anything else, LeeAnne trotted up to them.

"Could be nothing, but Mike's found a couple of kids hiding in that back alley over there who might have seen something," she explained when they turned to look at her.

Carley's phone rang. He pulled it out and glanced at the caller ID. "You can handle the interview, Taylor," he said. "Report back to me if there's anything useful."

Taylor's *duh* snort in reply went unnoticed as Carley hit the answer button and turned away with the phone held to his ear. Taylor left Carley to it and followed LeeAnne to the back of the parking lot where a narrow alley led between two of the shops. Trash cans filled the alley, but there was enough room to maneuver around them to get to where Mike was waiting. The area only smelled marginally better than the rotting parking lot behind them.

Mike's shoulders were rounded as if he were always protecting the back of his neck from an imminent threat. He was one of the most submissive wolves in Taylor's pack, more than happy to have a roof over his head, good food, and space to run. Taylor had originally found Mike in an alley similar to this one—starving and cowering away from any humans. Convincing Mike to come to the pack house hadn't been easy, but the wolf had bloomed as much as he probably ever would in the safety of Taylor's pack. Taylor ran a hand gently over one of Mike's shoulders as they reached him, and then Taylor stepped around Mike to see what he had found.

Two young men were leaning nonchalantly against the dirty alley wall. They smelled thickly of cigarette smoke, the acrid scent burning through Taylor's sensitive nose and forcing him not to get any closer. He could also smell the skunky, sickly scent of pot and something slick and oily that said there were harder drugs in their repertoire too. They didn't sneer at Taylor, but it was a near thing. Taylor could see the telltale curl of their lips beginning before they checked themselves.

"What did you see?" Taylor asked, hoping to get out of the smelly alley and away from the smelly humans as quickly as possible. Even he wouldn't begrudge a bath right about now.

The men stared first at Taylor's eyes, and when they couldn't hold his stare they looked at his ears. Taylor could almost see them deciding whether telling a Ge-Mi what they had seen was worth their time. Still, Taylor was used to this and knew how to be patient. Either they would make the decision to talk to Taylor anyway, or they would decide to run and Taylor would get to chase them down and force them to answer. Mike let out a low whine, and that sound seemed to galvanize them because one of the men finally opened his mouth to speak.

"We saw the body fall from the sky," the closer man said.

"We was on the roof," the second added. That meant they might have been close enough to see the car Antony was in.

"Body came flying down. Woooo, splat." The first man emphasized his words by dipping his hand in a downward curve in front of his face.

"Nah. It was more like woooo, crack," the second man cut in, his hand making the same awkward motion. "Body split open like an old trash bag." He kicked out at a nearby garbage can for emphasis, but his foot missed, and he staggered drunkenly for a second before his shoulder returned to the wall that was apparently propping them both up.

Taylor's hopes that they might be able to identify the car plummeted. He could guess why they had been up on that roof in the first place, and that guess went along with the pot and the oily smell of another drug. They were clearly high.

"Did you see the car that dropped him?" Taylor had to ask, if only to be thorough.

"It was big," the first man replied easily, but then he paused as if he had to think about that statement for a second. "Yeah, big."

"Two seats, four seats, bigger?" Taylor asked.

"Bigger. Took up the whole sky." The second man let out a giggle that he quickly stifled, his face immediately falling back into serious lines as he resumed his 'I hate Ge-Mis' stare that Taylor now knew was faked.

He wasn't going to get anything useful out of these yahoos. "Thank you for your time," he told them before turning around and starting to usher Mike and LeeAnne back out of the alley.

"I saw the driver," the first man called suddenly after Taylor had walked about five steps away. Taylor turned back around to look at him but didn't go any closer. He waited, and the first man obliged by continuing to speak. "He was all clean and shiny. Nice hair, you know." He made scissor-cutting motions with his fingers along the side of his face. "Looked kind of like that guy in the suit out there, you know?"

Taylor waited a few moments more to see if any new thought floated to the surface of the men's fried brains before nodding to them and resuming his trek out of the alley.

Chapter Two

Taylor showered and changed clothes at the pack house, then sat with his pack for the rest of the afternoon. He debriefed them on everything they had seen in that parking lot, which—aside from the body—hadn't been much, and then they hung out to play video games for the rest of the afternoon.

The pack only patrolled when there was an imminent threat to the city, like when the hyenas had been blowing up buildings. The rest of the time they were ready to get called out to help at any moment. That was the policy Lord Reyes had instituted when Taylor had first created his pack. They could stay and have secure housing, but they had to provide for the city the same as every citizen in Kensey did. The pack members hadn't been educated like Oliver or Taylor; they couldn't hide like Nevada had, and getting a regular job for most of them who were high-strung and jumpy really wasn't possible. A policing force of Ge-Mis was unique as far as Taylor was aware, but with their noses and their speed, they were able to keep crime in Kensey down.

Although he'd studied Ge-Mi history, Taylor had always wondered why more Ge-Mis didn't work in law enforcement. When Ge-Mis were first freed from the labs that created them, they tried to fit into society. Heck, society had even welcomed their new brothers and sisters. Unfortunately, there are bad apples in every bunch, and those Ge-Mis soon realized their extra abilities allowed them to commit crimes without being caught. A bear Ge-Mi could rip through walls, and no human had the equal strength to stop him. A cobra Ge-Mi could poison someone with a quick strike and slither away. The few history books remaining after the Great War were full of horror stories like that—of Ge-Mis doing bad things for bad reasons. There were no positive stories like doctor Ge-Mis saving lives due to their advanced sight. Those doctors were better able to see inside their patients during surgery. Nor were there any stories of Ge-Mi cops chasing bad guys with their faster speed and bringing them to justice. Only the bad stories survived, and they colored almost everything humans thought about Ge-Mis.

At least they did until Taylor's pack did start saving lives and catching criminals. And until Nevada had pulled off the scarf he wore to cover his ears and the populace of Kensey who had learned to love the quiet waiter realized what he was. Neither Nevada nor Ree bothered hiding what they were now, and the restaurant was still packed to the brim every night.

Ge-Mis needed more good stories to continue combatting the bad so maybe one day Ge-Mis would be considered people rather than animals.

Taylor loved his pack, and he enjoyed spending time with them, but as the sun began to dip below the tops of the nearby buildings, Taylor started itching to leave.

"Go find your cat," LeeAnne finally said when he shifted against her for what had to be the twelfth time. He wasn't going to wait to be told twice. Taylor squeezed out from where he was squished on the couch between LeeAnne and Drew—who both shifted over to share his spot—and went to go find his shoes.

Streetlights were just beginning to turn on as Taylor let himself out through the front gate of the tall fence that surrounded the pack house. He double-checked that the gate locked securely behind him before heading off into the city. It wasn't a far walk to Restaurant Spice, and when he got there, the building was as packed as usual. A glance at his watch told Taylor he was much too early. Nevada wouldn't get off for at least a half hour.

Taylor could feel his ears wilting at the thought, but then his stomach growled and he immediately perked up because now he had an excuse to go inside: he was a customer. The familiar, peculiar hush fell over the room as he stepped into the restaurant as people first saw his ears and tail and then remembered he was a Reyes. There was no way to tell which one scared them more.

Rosto, the restaurant owner, hurried over. It was good to see Rosto, who was another familiar figure from Taylor's childhood. Rosto had been childhood friends with Taylor's mother, and when she died he had done his best to step up and care for Taylor, along with Gramps and Carley. Also, since he was here, it meant Nevada would be able to leave on time. Nevada's familiar white head popped into view in the back of the restaurant near the drink station, so he was still very busy.

"If you give me a few minutes, I can have a table ready for you," Rosto said as he reached Taylor's side.

Taylor looked at the busy restaurant with every table full and a line of patrons trying not to glare at him for making their wait longer and shook his head.

"I'd prefer to order something to go that I can take with me when Nevada is done," he replied.

"Absolutely," Rosto said with a smile. "What are you in the mood for?"

"Everything's good here," Taylor admitted, which, given how poorly he had behaved the first few times he had been in the restaurant, wasn't a concession at all. "You know what we like."

Saying *we* sent a little thrill down Taylor's spine. He'd always had Gramps, and his pack had grown into another family of sorts, too, but Taylor hadn't known what wanting to—choosing to—create a new family with someone he cared for would be like.

Nevada walked around the low wall separating the kitchen from the restaurant. He was hefting a heavy tray of drinks, but as he turned, he caught sight of Taylor and immediately smiled. That thrill doubled, hitting Taylor low in his body in a way that wasn't entirely appropriate for a public location. Nevada turned away to deliver the drinks, and Taylor hoofed it through the arched doorway that separated the bright restaurant from the closed café, hoping Rosto would keep his too-knowing smile to himself.

The café lights were turned off when the café closed in the late afternoon and were only turned back on at night when the line for the restaurant was completely out the door and they needed somewhere out of bad weather to put the customers. The restaurant didn't use the tables since the health inspector hadn't approved the space for fine dining. The café was a dark, quiet space where Taylor could take a deep breath and get control over himself again.

An imperious meow from the back of the room alerted Taylor that he wasn't alone. There was a rustle as Hex climbed out of his basket and the soft pad of paws as he headed in Taylor's direction.

"Oh no, you don't," Taylor said with a growl in his voice. He stomped to the back of the café where Hex's basket was kept. Hex was the little menace that had attacked Taylor and incited him into stalking Nevada back to his apartment. Hex used to fit in the front pocket of Nevada's uniform shirt. He was the runt of his litter and tiny, but all kittens had to grow sometime. The tiny black kitten with a white stripe down his spine was now a slightly undersized-for-his-age kitten who could climb out of the basket he knew he wasn't supposed to leave.

Taylor intercepted Hex before he got more than a few feet from his basket, scooped Hex up, and deposited the disgruntled kitten right back in.

"You know better," Taylor said, his voice hard as he scolded.

Hex mewed at him piteously as if to say he was the innocent victim in this, but Taylor lifted his lip to show a little fang in response. Since he wasn't getting the sympathy he wanted, Hex let out an unhappy yowl and turned around in his basket so his back was facing Taylor.

"Yeah, well, if you hadn't gotten out of your basket, I would have come over to say hello without all this drama." Hex let out a little scoff at his words, but otherwise didn't turn around to acknowledge that Taylor was still in the same room as him. "Well, fine. See if I ever come say hi to you again."

Nevada's soft laughter came from the back of the shop where the kitchens of the two stores were connected. He walked into view a moment later carrying a plastic bag with two takeout containers inside.

It had only been a few weeks since the battle against the hyenas, but the changes in Nevada were amazing to see. He had been so shy—a hard worker and fierce when it came to his cats, but he never really looked people in the eye. There had been a moment during the battle where Nevada had looked around the restaurant and seen how many people were about to die, and he had ripped off the ratty bandana that had kept his adorable little ears concealed and dove into the fighting. Taylor had seen every moment of that fight on security video a couple days later, and he watched the tide immediately change against the hyenas.

Nevada had come out of that fight a new man, more confident in himself as a human and as a Ge-Mi, and it showed in how he conveyed himself now. His smile was still shy and nervous, but his shoulders were back and his head held high. The scarf was gone and his tail waved lazily behind him, now that he was done with work, and he wasn't flinching away from anyone else seeing his true self. It only made him more beautiful.

Taylor took the bag of food when Nevada held it out to him and waited while Nevada gently picked up Hex and draped the still-sulking kitten over his shoulder for the walk home.

"He's really getting too big for the shop," Nevada said with a sigh as he led the way out the door, "but I can't keep him home—there're too many other cats, and he never learned to share well—and he refuses to think about finding a new home."

They walked another block in silence, Nevada frowning pensively at Taylor's side and Taylor unable to think of an answer. Oddly enough, Taylor actually liked Hex. He had a take-it-or-leave-it relationship with the other cats in Nevada's hoard, but he didn't mind Hex, and when Hex wasn't sulking, he seemed to like Taylor too.

"Let him loose in the pack house." It was a crazy, radical thought, but Taylor couldn't take it back. There was no telling what the rest of the pack would think about sharing space with a cat, but Hex could hold his own. It might be worth it just to see Drew's reaction.

"We'll see how Hex feels about it in the morning," Nevada replied, which wasn't an answer, but was probably the best Taylor was going to get when Hex's butt was all he could see of the kitten at the moment.

Nevada scanned his finger at the front door to his apartment building and pulled the door open when it unlocked. They walked up the stairs together, and Taylor waited for Nevada to pull out the old key and get the door open. A chorus of happy meows greeted them. Maya and Beth were brown cats, but where Maya was thin and whippy looking, Beth was plump and matronly. Taylor knew Maya was only waiting for Hex to be ready to move on himself before she demanded a home of her own. She and Beth got along, but like Hex, Maya wasn't happy not in charge of her own home. Beth was the ruler of this house.

Or, at least, she believed she was.

Beth mewed imperiously when Nevada dropped Hex down to the floor, and Nevada ignored her long enough to grab dishes from the cabinets. Only once the table was set and Taylor could begin putting out their dinner did Nevada start dishing up bowls of cat food, including a smaller one full of kitten kibble for Hex.

They sat down to dinner together, and for the first few minutes their own chewing punctuated by the crunch of kibble was the only sound in the space. It was a pleasant way to spend an evening, but a bit too quiet for Taylor's taste.

"Looks like the restaurant is going well?" Taylor asked, hoping to start a conversation.

Nevada smiled at him and finished chewing before answering. "It's good. We're actually too busy. The kitchen staff can't handle the number of customers we're getting, and Rosto is hoping that by opening a second location across town we'll reduce the amount of people at the café while introducing new customers to our food."

"Sounds tricky. Splitting your customers like that won't hurt your overall revenue?"

Nevada shook his head. "Rosto hopes not. He's building on the opposite side of town and thinks that will be far enough apart that this location will only lose the customers traveling from over there."

"Sounds like a gamble, but it also sounds much more interesting than my day." Taylor grimaced at the reminder, but continued to cut into his chicken.

"You were too late to find Antony," Nevada stated with a grimace of his own. "How bad was it?"

"He's dead," Taylor replied, and his voice was firm enough to let Nevada know that he didn't want to explain how. Nevada got the message because he only shared a commiserating look with Taylor.

"So what's your next step?" he asked after they chewed for another minute in silence.

"Find out who killed him, if we can. The funeral will be in a few days. The entire family will be there, and I'm hoping to overhear some talk about anyone upset with Gramps for letting this happen."

"Lord Kensey will be there?" Nevada sounded concerned and Taylor understood why. Gramps was supposed to be in ill health—a fiction they had come up with after someone had poisoned him—and was a known target of their enemy. Taylor hadn't heard whether Gramps would be going, but—

"It would be an insult to Antony's family if Gramps didn't go," Taylor replied, wishing he had a better answer. "Carley will make sure security is tight, and I'll have my pack stationed around the perimeter too."

Nevada only nodded and carefully scraped his fork along his plate to scoop up the last of the sauce. He licked his fork clean with a satisfied purr, and Taylor had to look back down at his own almost-finished dinner. There was cute and then there was Nevada, and the sound of that innocent purr had Taylor repressing the need to toss the dishes to the side, push Nevada down onto the table, and do wicked and wonderful things.

But Nevada wasn't up to that just yet. It chafed that their relationship hadn't moved forward in that direction, but it only seemed to be bothering Taylor. Nevada hadn't noticed, as far as Taylor could tell. Part of it was definitely Nevada's innocence—which, admittedly, was one of the things Taylor liked most about him—but much more of it was about Nevada's ignorance. Yet, how did Taylor breech the idea of sex with Nevada? He could feel his tail and ears drooping at the thought of it.

"Do you mind cleaning up?" Nevada asked. He was leaning back in his chair looking content—like a cat that had gotten all the cream—and Beth hopped up into his lap for petting. "I want to shower before bed."

Taylor tried not to feel jealous. He stood and started gathering dishes. Washing them would take his mind off his carnal-leaning thoughts. Although, the mental image of Nevada, naked in the shower, would probably stick with him the entire time water from the sink was dripping down his hands.

"You've been dealing with dishes all day," Taylor replied truthfully. "I can handle this meal."

"Thanks," Nevada said. He sounded tired, but then he had been on his feet all day, running around a busy restaurant while catering to demanding customers. That Nevada enjoyed his job didn't make it any less tiring, just as Taylor being used to sniffing out culprits of murders, burglaries, and other criminal activity was something he enjoyed but would never get used to.

Beth sat patiently for a few more minutes of petting before abruptly deciding she had enough and hopping down from Nevada's lap. Taylor took his time clearing the table while Nevada gathered his energy to stand. He walked toward the bathroom and the waiting shower, and Taylor couldn't help watching that thick, beautiful tail waving behind Nevada's equally shapely ass until the door closed behind him.

Taylor tried to blank his mind as he rinsed the dishes and put them into the dishwasher and dumped all the trash into the can, which he made sure to cover tightly to keep out any curious cats. He wiped down the table and counters and was done well before Nevada despite how quick Nevada's showers always were.

He climbed the ladder up to Nevada's bedroom loft and undressed until he was only in his boxers. His tail wasn't too knotted since he had brushed it when he had showered earlier, but it was always good to get out any remaining tangles, so he picked up Nevada's brush from the top of the nearby dresser and got to work.

Nevada jumped up into the loft only a few minutes later and immediately saw Taylor holding the brush. His eyes lit up as if to say he really wanted Taylor to brush out his tail too, but his mouth remained firmly shut.

Clearly, they had a problem with talking about things they wanted. Taylor couldn't ask Nevada about doing anything sexual, and Nevada couldn't even ask for Taylor's help with a little grooming. It was disheartening to realize, but it was also something that was possible for them to work toward.

"You can ask me anything, you know," Taylor said softly. He waved the brush through the air between them to show what he meant. "I won't bite you."

"Not anymore, at least," Nevada added with a small grin.

"Not unless you ask me to," Taylor finished and was gratified when Nevada's cheeks immediately tinted pink, and he bashfully dropped his gaze down to look at the brush.

He turned his body so his damp tail, sticking out of the back of his boxers, was facing Taylor. "Could you..." he trailed off.

Taylor took pity on him, but he also didn't want to wait to have a chance to stroke his hands down the thickly muscled and very fluffy tail. Brushing Nevada's tail was a soothing motion for them both, even when the tines got caught in a knot, and Taylor fell into the rhythm of it.

Nevada was purring and chuffing happily after the first few strokes, and Taylor watched as Nevada's spine went boneless and he sank into their bed of pillows and blankets.

For the next few minutes, Taylor ran his fingers and the brush through Nevada's silky fur, marveling at how soft the white-and-black strands were against his skin. The knots didn't take long to brush out, and after that it was like a massage to them both. Except, Taylor wanted to touch more.

His free hand drifted upward until the tips of his fingers could brush along Nevada's back where a shorter layer of fur ran up his spine. Nevada's shoulders tensed and the purring stopped, but he didn't tell Taylor to stop. In fact, the way Nevada's shoulders quivered told Taylor he wanted those fingers to continue stroking this new, uncharted territory.

Taylor moved slowly, using his fingertips and the barest pressure to trace one of the rosettes on Nevada's back. He moved on to another one, going higher up Nevada's back and forcing him to lean over Nevada until his chest was pressed against Nevada's back.

The brush was forgotten, lost somewhere off the side of the bed, as Taylor used two hands to smooth over Nevada's shoulders and up his neck to where his feathery hair hung long and uneven. And then, suddenly, Nevada was shifting underneath Taylor, rolling over and forcing Taylor to sit up slightly. They were chest to chest when Nevada stopped, and Nevada's hands came up to grip Taylor's.

Nevada's eyes were wide with confusion and...lust. His pupils were blown open, and he was panting slightly, yet that confusion said he didn't understand why. No, Nevada understood his body's reaction, Taylor corrected himself. He was an adult male, after all, and there were some things men figured out just fine on their own as teenagers. What Nevada didn't understand was why he was reacting like that in response to Taylor. He didn't comprehend that his body could react to someone else's touch.

Now Taylor felt like a dirty old man taking advantage of a child. He tried to pull away, but Nevada's fingers tightened.

"Please," Nevada said softly. "I want..." He paused, and Taylor could see his newfound courage and resolve take the fore and allow him to continue. "I want you. I want this. I just don't know..." he trailed off again.

"I'm your first relationship," Taylor said softly, knowing it was true because who else before him would have been okay with the tail and the ears? Who else would Nevada have trusted with seeing his true self? "We can take it slow and learn together."

Nevada nodded firmly. "That's what I need. I want to... I want to know more—to do more. With you. I just don't know what that entails."

The confusion had faded, replaced by an earnest, yet shy mien that Taylor wanted to lick off of Nevada's face. He wanted to lick a lot more than Nevada's face. He controlled himself but couldn't help dipping his head lower. Taylor didn't say something cliché like "That's why I'm here" or "Let me teach you," but it was definitely implied as he brushed his lips over Nevada's.

Nevada let out a growling chuff as Taylor pulled away. Taylor obeyed that demand and pushed close again, pressing their lips together firmly enough that a shot of electricity went down his spine and fluffed out his tail. Nevada's hips arched upward, and Taylor obeyed that wordless demand for more.

And then there wasn't room for thinking at all, only sensation and emotion amid panting and purrs.

Chapter Three

There was nothing redeeming about a suit. Sure, he looked professional, but the damned thing was so uncomfortable, Taylor couldn't imagine someone having the mental capacity to conduct business. He would be completely distracted by the tight tie constricting his neck and the stiff pants and jacket keeping his legs and arms from moving properly. He wouldn't be able to run while wearing this.

His only consolation was that everyone around him was similarly dressed. Gramps and Carley were standing with him, so Taylor didn't dare reach up to tug on the knot in his tie. Rosto and Nevada walked up to the graveside together. Rosto had driven Nevada to the cemetery because Nevada's apartment was on his way, whereas Taylor had needed to go home to the Reyes mansion to pick up his suit and had ridden with the car leaving from there.

Nevada didn't own a suit and there hadn't been time to get him one, but he had a new pair of slacks with a tail hole and a button-up shirt that he had pulled from the bottom of a drawer beneath his usual wear of frayed shirts or work attire. His hair was brushed and he had borrowed some of the gel Taylor had left at his apartment, so it was styled around his little ears in a way that had Taylor almost wishing they had more—happier—opportunities to dress up. Maybe if Taylor found one where he didn't have to wear a tie or jacket, it might be fun.

Antony's family walked up next. His mother was in tears and had to be supported by her stoic-looking husband. If his eyes weren't red-tinged, Taylor might have thought he didn't care, but Antony's father had been equally as devastated as his mother when he'd received the news of Antony's death.

Carley seemed to be fairly certain they weren't part of the coup attempt. Neither had the money nor the political ambition to want the Reyes crown, and they weren't dumb enough to get duped into helping. Yet Antony had learned to hate Ge-Mis from somewhere, and given how both parents nodded politely to Gramps, but pointedly ignored Taylor next to him, Taylor had a good idea where that attitude had stemmed from.

Nevada's hand crept into his and squeezed his fingers comfortingly. Antony's feelings toward the Ge-Mi—as echoed by his parents' actions—were an old pain for Taylor, one he had long gotten used to ignoring. Still, it felt nice that someone not only understood what Taylor was feeling, but empathized with that hurt. Taylor couldn't help gently squeezing Nevada's hand in return, and he kept hold of it as the last of the mourners found seats and the graveside service began.

The casket was closed, of course, but someone had set up an easel where a datapad was slowly scrolling through pictures of Antony from childhood to present. The flowers piled on and around the casket were cloyingly sweet and likely strong enough that even the human noses around him could smell it.

Traitor Antony might have been, but he was still a Reyes. His grave was inside the Reyes private cemetery outside the city, but it was on the outskirts along the fence, where only those out of favor with the current ruling family of Kensey were buried. The officiant leading the service was the same one who would lead any of the funerals for the assembled family—Gramps included— and no expense had been spared for the dark wood coffin or the flowers.

The officiant started quickly once everyone was assembled, and Taylor sang along with the hymns and listened to him speak about a young man whose life was lost too soon. Then it was time for people who knew Antony well to get up and speak about him. School friends, coworkers, and even his ex-girlfriend all stood and talked about what a wonderful, caring, and hardworking man Antony had been.

It wasn't that Taylor disagreed with any of that, but the Antony he knew was cold, sneering, and always had a fist or a kick ready for his younger cousin. Antony had managed to conceal that ugly part of him away from everyone else, reserving it for Taylor and likely for any other Ge-Mis he met. It wasn't right, but it was life for

Taylor and Antony was dead now because of it. Taylor could put it behind him no matter how much it rankled.

Then Antony's mother stood up to speak. "My son was such a happy boy. Always smiling, always reaching out to help others. Everyone here has said what I already knew: everyone loved Antony. What happened to him was senseless, an act of hatred perpetrated on him by enemies of the Reyes family. He didn't deserve this ending, but I hope wherever he is now, he is safe and happy and can forget this terrible thing he went through."

Taylor sat through her speech calmly and felt Gramps doing the same thing on his other side because Gramps didn't move or shift around while she was talking. They both had their stoic, public faces on. The thing was, most of what she said was true. Antony was killed by an enemy of the Reyes family, but her implication that the reason he had been targeted was his family name was wrong, and—despite the fact that only a select few knew why he had died—everyone at the funeral knew it had nothing to do with his name. The fence line so nearby was all the evidence they needed to understand Gramps considered Antony at least an outcast, if not an outright traitor, and there was also the fact that when the officiant briefly turned to look at Gramps, Gramps declined to stand to offer his own words about Antony.

The funeral ended quickly after that, with the attendants lowering Antony's body into the grave as the mourners began to slowly trickle out of the cemetery. Antony's mother was so bereft, she was supported the whole way back to her car. Taylor remained behind with

Gramps, Nevada, Rosto, and Carley to let the crowds clear, mostly for security reasons. Taylor finally took a deep breath now clear of the perfume and cologne of the rest of the mourners. The scent of the freshly dug earth of the grave was strongest, followed by his favorite smell that was purely Nevada. The rest of their little group mixed in, but those smells were familiar too, as were the faint scents of those of his pack who were upwind.

If they hadn't been in the middle of a cemetery, being outside together would have been a pleasant way to spend an afternoon. He and Nevada needed to sneak off and have a picnic somewhere—that was what the day felt like, at least. If they found somewhere private enough, maybe the picnic blanket could be used for more than one thing.

He was never so glad to be sitting on his tail, Taylor mused as he tried to wrench his thoughts back to a more appropriate topic for a public venue. The darn thing would still be wagging furiously after a thought like that.

Taylor needed to focus on something else, like the reason why he was at a grave in the first place. It had to have been someone Antony trusted. Not the person who killed him, but whoever had recruited him into the coup. There were plenty of people—family and not—that coveted Gramps's position and hated that Gramps had chosen Taylor as his heir. Antony was only one cousin of many possibilities Gramps could have chosen for a blood heir that wasn't Ge-Mi and someone out there was no doubt aiming for exactly that to happen.

The first attempt to kill Gramps via poison had failed, but it had not only forced Taylor to take up his leadership role as the heir—it had forced the people he was suddenly working with to acknowledge he was not only competent, but he could and did make a good Reyes. The enemy must know that attempt had failed, and Taylor had no doubt their next plan would be much more thorough.

So, what did killing Antony so brutally and so publicly have to do with it?

Taylor huffed out a breath, upset because he had absolutely zero idea. Carley was the big thinker of their group. Nevada was too, of course, but Nevada needed to focus on learning his new role in the restaurant. He didn't need the aggravation of Taylor's family drama intruding any more than it already had.

He took in a slow breath and let it out again, then paused and took in another quick sniff of air. It smelled like cat, but a different sort of cat smell to Nevada.

Where? Taylor growled and stood, and he knew his team would have noticed his attention. He sniffed the air again, trying to pinpoint where upwind the scent was coming from. Not from behind the line of headstones leading away from Antony's grave. Taylor turned. Not from behind the massive mausoleum that took up a very large section of the middle of the cemetery.

"The tree," Nevada whispered.

Taylor turned again and saw what Nevada must have. There were large, ornamental trees lining the walk, and up in the tree closest to them was a dark spot of color that didn't belong. With a few quick hand signals, Taylor had his pack tighten their patrol. He didn't have them come closer just in case this was a distraction. With Nevada and Carley at his back, Taylor had enough backup to handle this.

Rosto and Gramps started casually walking toward the path, idly chatting about the weather. Carley walked a few hundred feet ahead of them, and the hand farthest from the tree was tucked out of sight. Taylor and Nevada both ranged farther out, seeming to be taking a random path through the headstones, but both were still heading toward that tree.

Gramps took the path closer to the mausoleum while saying something to Rosto about paying his respects to his parents since he was here already. That got him safely out of the way, and Taylor could see LeeAnne behind one of the columns where she could keep an eye out for more trouble. That left them the tree.

Nevada came up from the far side of the tree while Taylor came from the front. Carley stood behind and to the right of Taylor, where the laser gun he was holding would back them up.

"Who's up there?" Taylor asked, a growl vibrating hard through his chest.

"A petitioner." The voice was silky and spoken almost like a purr. A long black tail poked down from the lowest branch, followed by a foot clad in a ratty tennis shoe. The man who followed looked and smelled clean, but the rest of him was as unkempt as that shoe. His jeans had holes in the knees, and the cuffs were completely frayed. The hemline of his shirt had come lose, and one of the armpits had a hole in it. He was covered head to toe in short, deep-black fur, and his ears on top of his head were rounded, but longer than Nevada's. He was a Ge-Mi panther, probably a black leopard variety.

"A petitioner," Taylor repeated, trying not to sound skeptical.

The man nodded. "I tried to get in at the mansion, but I don't have money for nicer clothes, and I don't know anyone who could get me in, anyway. I figured I could ask permission to live in this city from you directly, so I followed you here."

"Come down now!" Nevada called suddenly. Taylor had to stifle his surprised jump, instead narrowing his eyes at the panther in front of him.

"What are you hiding?" Taylor made his voice sharp with warning, and he knew his ears and tail were broadcasting aggression.

"I'm not...please don't hurt him!" Panic had the panther's eyes widening, and he held his hands out in front of him as if to show he was unarmed. "Shaw, come on down."

A second ratty pair of sneakers popped out from the tree, followed by a second panther Ge-Mi, who promptly hid himself against the first one's back. Taylor caught enough of a glimpse of the second cat—Shaw—to tell they looked similar enough they were at least brothers, if not twins.

"Are there any more of you up there?" Taylor had to ask.

The first panther shook his head in denial. "Only me and Shaw. I'm Craw."

Taylor took a deep breath to check for scents, but all he smelled were the two of them. Nevada walked around the tree, stopping at an angle to Shaw and Craw so he didn't block Carley's shot. They were shy like Mike. Taylor understood that, but it took a second for his adrenaline to fade so he could switch hats and be a Reyes rather than a wolf.

Mike hadn't been able to petition directly to stay in the city. He had been too afraid of showing up at the doors as a Ge-Mi, and he hadn't felt he had anything to offer that would convince the lord of the city to let him stay. When Taylor had found him in the back of that alley, poor Mike had been scrounging for food in a dumpster. Craw and Shaw weren't far off from that point, but Taylor couldn't let pity color his decision either.

"This city has one rule," Taylor told them, his voice firm but gentle, rather than growling. Craw's ears perked up at the change in tone, but he didn't otherwise move. "We only accept newcomers who are willing and able to contribute. Everyone holds down a job, pays their taxes, and is a productive member of society. You want to stay here, you need to prove you can do that too."

"How?" Craw asked, his voice hopeful.

Taylor shrugged. "Depends on what skills you have." He didn't have much hope for Shaw, who was quivering with fear and hadn't spoken yet, but if Craw could earn enough for them both, then it wouldn't be the first time the city accepted a dependent who couldn't contribute.

Craw grinned happily, showing a bit of fang, but it wasn't aggressive. Still, Taylor lifted his lip as if to say he had fangs, too, so don't mess with him. Craw's lips immediately closed, but his smile didn't fade.

"I'm good for any hard labor you need. Construction, moving. If it's got heavy lifting, I'm your guy."

A skill Taylor knew they didn't really need more people for, and it didn't lead to a large enough salary to take care of Shaw.

"But Shaw's the one you really want," Craw continued. "Put him in a kitchen and magic happens. He's a classically trained chef."

"You're a chef!" Nevada gasped, and Taylor immediately knew the matter was ended. Restaurant Spice was looking for a new chef for when the new restaurant opened. They hadn't been able to find someone as good as the current chef, who unfortunately couldn't be in two places at once.

"There is a restaurant looking for a new chef right now," Taylor explained. "Shaw has a week to audition for the position, and if he is hired, you'll both get six months of probation. Both of you hold down a job and keep your noses clean for those six months and you'll be fine."

"And if Shaw isn't hired at this restaurant?" Craw asked.

This time when Taylor showed a bit of fang, he meant it. "He has a week. If there's another restaurant willing to take him, I'll still consider your petition."

"You hear that, Shaw?" Craw turned his back to Taylor and put his hands gently on Shaw's shoulders. "You and me, we're going to get jobs and we'll have a real home. It's going to be amazing." Shaw nodded and brushed his forehead against Craw's chest. Craw turned his head to look at Taylor. "Where does Shaw have to be for the audition?"

Taylor looked over at Nevada, who grinned at him before turning his attention to Shaw. "It's called Restaurant Spice. Come by around noon, and we'll get you set up with a test to see what you can do."

"Thank you," Craw replied for them both because Shaw apparently didn't talk. He nodded politely to Taylor and draped an arm over Shaw's shoulders as they both started walking to the exit.

Once they were out of sight, Carley holstered his gun and joined them. "Curious that we're looking for a potential implant from another city who might have killed Antony, and they show up right after the funeral." Carley was looking down the path where Craw and Shaw had just vanished, but Taylor saw his lips compress into a thoughtful frown. "It seems a bit too obvious to me, but you never know. I'll see if I can dig a little deeper into their background than we usually do for petitioners."

"Did you look for my background too?" Nevada asked. Taylor walked closer, and his tail started waving lazily behind him when Nevada immediately pressed his shoulder into Taylor's side. They walked with their arms brushing, heading toward the mausoleum.

"Of course, but all we found was a young kid leaving his previous city, likely escaping the memories of his recently deceased mother. Princess notwithstanding, you really didn't do anything to raise any red flags for us." Carley paused to frown at Nevada briefly. "Except for the fact that you're a Ge-Mi. Somehow we missed that entirely."

Nevada giggled. "I worked hard for that, but I'm really glad I don't have to pretend to be human any longer."

Taylor was, too, but they reached the mausoleum before he could say so out loud. Gramps and Rosto were waiting inside the doors with LeeAnne standing barely out of sight on the far side of the building.

"You can tell me about it in the car," Gramps told Taylor the second they were close enough not to have to yell. "Rosto and Nevada have a restaurant to run, so let them go before this day drags on any longer."

Taylor turned to Nevada, who was already grinning at him. Nevada bopped Taylor on the arm with his tail, and his smile deepened in a way that had Taylor's thoughts spinning off work and back into the bedroom. But then, Nevada turned and walked off toward the front gates with Rosto.

Taylor watched him go, feeling his tail drooping down to hang between his legs the farther Nevada got, until he climbed into the passenger seat of Rosto's car and they flew off.

"You have got it bad," Gramps said softly. His hand came to rest on Taylor's shoulder, and his fingers squeezed. "Come on. You can see him again tonight. We need to focus on our own work now too. The city isn't going to run itself."

He led the way to the waiting car and driver, pulling Taylor and Carley along in his wake. Taylor took one last look at Nevada's retreating car, let out a huff, and signaled to his pack that they were moving out. Gramps was right: it was time for everyone to get to work.

Chapter Four

Waking up next to Nevada was a rare treat, one Taylor wasn't about to ruin. Usually, he was the one running out, or not able to stay over. Nevada had the steady job with fairly steady hours while Taylor could be called out at all hours of the day and night. Nevada never begrudged Taylor's phone going off, or Taylor having to leave, nor did he seem to mind that there were still plenty of nights Taylor slept at the pack house.

Taylor hated that. He wanted to spend all day and all night curled up with Nevada. Every once in a while, though, he got the entire night and morning, and that was time to cherish.

Nevada was still asleep, curled up into a ball with his knees pressed to his chest. One arm and his tail were flung over Taylor, who usually slept sprawled on his back. With Nevada curled into Taylor's side like that, Taylor didn't dare move. Instead he inhaled the heady scent of their personal smells so perfectly mixed together in the small loft space.

Despite everything else going on in his life, Taylor knew he would be happy if he could spend the rest of his days lying here, just like this.

Nevada let out a rumbling yawn and stretched out of his curl so the length of his body pressed against the length of Taylor's. Nevada's sleepy eyes blinked open, and he turned to look up at Taylor.

"Morning," Nevada said, his voice low and rough from sleep.

"Good morning to you too," Taylor replied, and his own voice was low and growling, but for a totally different reason. Nevada's eyes widened for a moment in surprise, and then he smiled, and that was all Taylor needed. He rolled over so his body was pressing Nevada down into their nest, and rational thought deserted them both for a while.

*

Waking up a second time with Nevada was even better, especially since their smells had combined so much more. They both needed to get up and shower so they could head to their respective jobs for the day, but Taylor still didn't want to move.

Some suspicious rustling noises came from below them. Actually, just the fact that there wasn't a lot of crying or mewing coming from down there was suspicious. Taylor was about to force himself to get up to investigate when Nevada let out a low growl and rolled over so he could look over the edge of his sleeping loft.

"Do it, and I won't take you to see your new home," Nevada said with a snarl.

The answering mewl sounded young, which, combined with Nevada's statement, made Taylor think Hex was up to something again. Hex hadn't just outgrown Nevada's front pocket and his basket; he was outgrowing Nevada's admittedly small apartment. He was a cat that needed multiple rooms to explore and to keep him too busy to get into trouble.

"I was going to take you there after work if you behaved all day," Nevada continued, "but you're not off to a good start."

There was a thump as Hex jumped off whatever he had climbed onto and then let out a pointed meow as if to say, "Who, me?"

Nevada snorted, but he rolled over onto his back and turned his head so he was facing Taylor.

"Sorry, I should have asked you first if tonight was okay."

Taylor grinned. "I'm looking forward to it. That ankle biter is going to give my pack the wake-up they didn't know they needed." His lips lifted even more into what he knew was probably a rather evil smile. Nevada laughed and rolled over again so he was pressed against Taylor. He took a quick kiss, a bare peck of his lips against Taylor's, before levering himself to his feet and heading over to the drawers to find clothes for the day.

"Now I have to take another shower," he grumbled, irritably picking at something that had gotten stuck in his tail. Except, a moment later, his smile returned. He jumped down from the loft and vanished into the bathroom before that smile could do more than briefly remind Taylor of what they had been doing not too long ago.

Taylor hopped in the shower once Nevada was done, and they ate a quick breakfast of cold cereal over the sink after Taylor was also dressed. A big plastic bag was waiting by the door. Taylor could see an extra litter box, some litter, a bag of food, and Hex's bowls inside. Hex himself was waiting there, too, sitting patiently with a small toy mouse in his mouth.

They rinsed their bowls and left them in the sink before they both grabbed their wallets and got ready to leave. Taylor hefted the bag while Nevada draped Hex over his shoulders. Nevada locked his door behind them as they headed off to work.

*

Taylor entered the Reyes mansion via a side door. He left the bag of supplies on a small table there before heading into the depths of the building. The private living areas were on the top floor, with public meeting rooms the next two floors down. The first floor was purely for the administrative staff that kept the city running. Gramps had an office there where he usually spent the day. The basement was where a lot of the real work was done. Taylor found the correct staircase and let the system scan his DNA. The door unlocked and he walked downstairs.

At the bottom of the staircase was what Taylor liked to refer to as the maze. There were hallways branching off in all directions heading to rooms and offices for the various, more covert needs of the city. Carley's office was down here, for example.

Taylor went into the maze, familiar with his path, and a few minutes later walked into the largest computer lab. Carley was sitting at one of the long tables, tapping at the holographic keyboard. Two more people were sitting with him, helping to manipulate whatever data was displayed above their sitting-height heads.

"Your new cat Ge-Mis have an interesting history," Carley said as Taylor sat in one of the empty chairs. "They come from far west in a city called Los Gatos—ironic, I know—but it turns out it wasn't particularly cat friendly. At least, not Ge-Mi friendly. The lord there kept them as a sort of sideshow. He forced them to perform for money. Acrobatics and the like. They escaped when they were fifteen and ended up starting their journey east."

Carley reached out to turn one of the images floating above them, and Taylor saw two younger versions of Shaw and Craw, Shaw still partially hidden behind Craw.

"They stopped in Vegas, which I know you've heard of before," Carley continued.

Of course Taylor had heard of Vegas. It was the far west version of Morse, the city the hyenas had come from. It was completely lawless, but it was also a haven for Ge-Mis trying to escape from cities where the lords were abusive to them. If what Carley had said about the lord of Gatos was true, then it made sense for Shaw and Craw to travel there.

"Shaw got a job washing dishes at some hole-in-the-wall where Craw was doing the stocking work. For the next five or so years, they worked there as Shaw continued to learn in the kitchen. When they moved on, they continued east—I assume stopping whenever they needed money since I've been able to track them thus far via Shaw's employment."

Carley reached upward again, but this time he pressed to open a file and a line of images popped out and began to rotate around the computer hologram sphere. It was as if someone had taken a dozen pictures of Antony's body, but each time his body was in a totally different location.

Each picture showed a body that had been dropped from a significant height, but more importantly, each body had been gutted in a straight line from chest to abdomen.

"In every city we've been able to track them, we also found a death in this manner." Carley sounded completely certain, which meant he had the research to back his statement up.

"Could be someone trying to frame them," one of Carley's assistants added.

"This many coincidences is too much of a pattern." Carley shook his head as he closed the file and brought up a picture of Craw and Shaw from the city's surveillance.

"That said, I've had them tailed since the cemetery, and all they've done is sleep in an alley last night, clean up this morning in a public restroom, and head to the restaurant a few minutes ago. My guess is Rosto is probably going to hire them both. Craw could do as a waiter, so if Shaw is as good a chef as he claims, there's no reason not to. This way we can keep a better eye on them, anyway."

Which was likely the real reason Rosto would hire them, although Rosto wouldn't hurt the restaurant by hiring someone who couldn't actually cook. If Shaw wasn't as good a chef as Craw claimed, they would have to find some other means of either keeping them close, or of kicking them out of the city.

"Any idea how long they've actually been here?" Taylor asked. They knew when Antony had been killed, but had Shaw and Craw actually been in the city then?

Carley let out a heavy sigh. "We have no idea. We have them on camera trying to get into the mansion two days before the funeral, according to the guard they spoke with to request permission to stay in the city, and we've been trying to backtrack via the surveillance system, but they keep ducking into back alleys where we lose them."

So they were confirmed to be in the city within a day or so of Antony's death. Taylor frowned up at the picture of the twins up on the screen.

"I'm interested in knowing what all the people killed have in common. If Shaw and Craw are working for someone, then all the dead people managed to get in the way of that someone."

Carley steepled his hands in front of his mouth as he thought. "Or they're assassins for hire, and the people they've killed mean nothing to us. Still, it's worth looking into." His eyes went to his left, and the assistant sitting there nodded and started typing.

Taylor leaned back in his chair, looking up at the hologram of the computer screen as if something in the files up there would magically provide the answer. "Have you isolated any suspicious payments in Antony's bank accounts or gotten any closer to who he might be working for?"

"You know I haven't, or I would have told you first thing," Carley replied shortly. "Why don't you hop on a terminal and try looking for yourself? You know where to find the spreadsheet of what we've already tried."

Carley wasn't wrong. Taylor would prefer to be out on the streets trying to sniff out the culprit that way, but without even the barest scent to start from, there was no point in even trying to go hunting. He had to find something first. It was going to require sitting still for a while, which wasn't going to be fun.

Taylor got up from his chair and moved to an empty computer, knowing his tail might be between his legs, but his ears were sharply pointed in anticipation of finding something.

Chapter Five

Nevada walked out of Restaurant Spice right on time, which meant Rosto must be there today. Hex was draped over his shoulder, but he looked eager to get wherever they were going. Nevada smiled immediately when he saw Taylor leaning against the wall across the street, and Taylor felt his tail start wagging automatically in response. He pushed off the wall and walked over to Nevada, who offered his hand for Taylor to take.

"How was work?" Taylor asked as they walked together down the street.

Nevada grinned happily at him. "We finally have a new chef that can keep up. Shaw has to learn all of our recipes, but he definitely knows what he's doing. And with Craw as our new waiter, it won't be a problem for Ree to start at the new restaurant when it opens." He sounded really excited and was practically skipping down the sidewalk.

Taylor opened his mouth to tell Nevada the truth about Shaw and Craw, but closed it a second later. Nevada seemed so happy about the recent developments at the restaurant. It wasn't worth ruining that, not even to tell Nevada for his own protection. Nevada didn't need to know about all the deaths or about their suspicions that Shaw and Craw might be involved with the murderers. He just needed to be safe.

"Do me a favor and don't go anywhere alone with those guys until we finish their background checks," Taylor finally said. "That's why we impose a probationary period on all new residents, just in case we find something in their history. It can take a while, and finding the full information for Ge-Mis is especially difficult because they don't often have proper records."

"Er...I promised to go apartment hunting with them tomorrow," Nevada admitted.

Taylor let out a helpless laugh. Trust Nevada to make friends with possible serial killers.

"You know, Shaw doesn't talk much—or at all, really—but he seems nice," Nevada continued. "And Craw's friendly. I think you'd like them."

He didn't know the truth. Taylor had to remind himself of that fact.

"Nevada," Taylor began slowly, trying to figure out how to say it now that the time to actually tell Nevada the truth had passed. "We've started their background checks, and it doesn't look good."

Nevada frowned at him, and Taylor felt his ears and tail droop at the knowledge that he had ruined Nevada's happy vibe.

"Don't be jealous. You know I have friends other than you, and my making two new ones isn't going to hurt us."

Taylor gaped at him. "That wasn't... I wasn't saying that at all!"

Nevada grinned at Taylor and whapped him in the back with his tail. "I know. Tell me next time. Don't hide things from me to keep me safe."

This time his ears and tail drooped with shame, but then Nevada squeezed his hand. Taylor took a deep breath and picked up where he left off.

"All these deaths happening at the same time in the same cities, where Shaw and Craw were living, is too much of a coincidence," he finished. "We don't have concrete proof, of course, but Carley seems certain."

Nevada hummed. "Have you thought about just asking them?"

"That would give away both the fact that we looked and that we have the resources to dig into activity in other lords' domains," Taylor replied immediately, although he had to admit it wasn't exactly a bad idea. Confront them straight out, get it all in the open, and see if any information pops out. It had to be better than sitting at a desk staring fruitlessly at a computer all day. "If we keep the way we found out about it secret, maybe it won't be a problem. I'll tell Carley about it, and we can ask them tomorrow when we're out looking for an apartment."

Nevada let out a breath. "A whole new level of anxiety never before applied to the stress of finding somewhere to live. Okay. We can figure it out."

"I have to tell Carley first. If he says no, we'll have to forget it." Taylor looked down at Nevada and had to stifle a laugh. He knew that particular set to Nevada's chin. It was the same one as the day Nevada had stubbornly watched him try to jump up into the loft, completely ignoring the laws of gravity as he did so. Regardless of what Carley said, the question was going to get asked tomorrow.

They reached the pack house before Taylor could think of a way to argue with Nevada's expressive chin. Taylor scanned his finger and held the gate open for Nevada and Hex, and they walked up to the front door together. It was flung open before Taylor could reach the handle, and Drew pointed his finger at Hex.

"Are you crazy? Don't bring that thing in here!"

LeeAnne dropped her hand over Drew's finger and pushed it down. "He saw the bag of supplies you left."

"You went through my stuff!" Taylor yelped. "That was mine."

"It reeked of cat. I had to go through it." Drew sniffed, but he spun around and stomped off into the house instead of continuing to confront Taylor directly. He apparently felt he had disobeyed his alpha enough for one day while still conveying his disquiet effectively.

"This is going to go well. I can tell," LeeAnne muttered under her breath, sarcasm dripping from every word. "Come on then," she continued in a louder voice. "Best to get this over with."

Taylor and Nevada followed her inside, and Taylor shut the front door firmly. He liked the idea of fierce little Hex living in this house with the pack—and he knew Hex was entirely capable of handling all the wolves—but Taylor wasn't certain he was up to the turmoil dropping a kitten in with a bunch of dogs was going to cause. Oh well. It was too late to change his decision.

"What do we need to do to get Hex set up?" Taylor asked Nevada once they had taken their shoes off and headed farther into the house.

"Show him where his litter box and his food bowl will be kept, and for the most part Hex will take care of himself." Nevada swung Hex down from his shoulder and held him up at head height so they could look each other in the eye. "I know you have good manners. I suggest you use them."

Hex meowed back, and Taylor heard the usual kitten-style derision that meant Hex had to be reminded to behave at every opportunity. Nevada rolled his eyes, but an adorable little grin lifted his lips as he gently put Hex on the floor.

Hex strolled off ahead of them, nose twitching as he looked around his new home. He vanished around the corner, and only then did Nevada's smile fade into a pensive frown.

"He'll be okay," Taylor said softly. He reached out and pulled Nevada into a hug, glad when Nevada came willingly and dropped his head onto Taylor's shoulder. "He tried to kill me the first time we met. I'm sure he can handle the rest of the pack too."

Nevada's fluffy little ear twitched as the breath from Taylor's speaking touched it, and it was right there. So enticingly close. All Taylor had to do was bend his neck forward just a touch...

Nevada let out a shocked yowl when Taylor nipped the curve of his ear and jumped out of Taylor's arms, which was the only disappointing part of this particular game. Taylor grinned happily at Nevada's affronted expression and bounced slightly on the balls of his feet, ready to chase, and catch, and maybe do a little more nipping in some more sensitive spots.

"Augh!"

Taylor sighed and let the excitement drain from his body. Nevada was pensively looking over his shoulder in the direction of Drew's yell, his lower lip caught enticingly between his teeth.

"Let's check it out," Taylor said, his voice heavy with disappointment. He would much rather be chasing Nevada up the stairs, only to catch him and drag him into Taylor's bedroom. Nevada wouldn't enjoy that, though, at least, not until he knew Hex was okay. They walked together down the hall and into the living room.

The overstuffed couches were full of his pack members, most of whom were stifling laughter behind a hand or, in LeeAnne's case, laughing outright. They were all looking at Drew, who had taken his usual place in the center of the couch. Drew's hands were in the air, and his eyes and mouth were wide in panic. Taylor rounded the couch and immediately saw why. Hex had jumped into

Drew's lap, curled up, and started purring. An asshole as only a cat could be. Taylor couldn't help rolling his eyes at the sight.

Hex would be fine here; that was certain. There were much more important things to worry about besides whether Hex was setting in. At the same time, it really was little things like Hex not giving a shit that Drew wasn't happy that made Taylor's tail wag. Nevada snickered and leaned against Taylor's side to watch, and that was another little thing that would keep him going the next time he was stuck in the basement digging hopelessly for any little clue. Still, they had to make plans for tomorrow. Taylor wanted at least half the pack within howling distance while they were apartment hunting, and he needed to call Carley to ensure they even had permission to confront Shaw and Craw. Or, more likely, to tell Carley what Nevada was going to do, regardless of whether permission was granted, so Carley could be prepared for any potential fallout.

He had better get all of that ready now before he got distracted again. Taylor rubbed his cheek against Nevada's head before slowly pulling away. He pulled out his phone in answer to Nevada's curious look and left the living room, happy to abandon Drew to his fate.

Chapter Six

Taylor had never realized how grateful he was to have avoided ever living in an apartment building. Between the Reyes mansion and the pack house, he always had a place to sleep where he wasn't surrounded on all sides by strangers. Apartments smelled like strangers, from their personal scent to their cooking and their trash, and it was deeply unpleasant.

He couldn't blame Shaw and Craw from turning down the first three apartments they had toured so far.

Taylor didn't know why he had never noticed the smell of other humans in close proximity at Nevada's place before, although Nevada only had one very quiet neighbor on his floor, the entire place smelled of cats, and Taylor admittedly always had something else on his mind when he went there. Nevada had that effect on him, even when Taylor had first gone there ready to tear Nevada apart.

"Ree recommended this next place," Nevada was telling Shaw and Craw. The three of them were walking together a little ahead of Taylor. "It was a full suite for the homeowner's mother, but she recently died. The homeowner converted the suite into a rental apartment. It's technically only a one-bedroom, but Ree said there's a den with a door that could be used as a second bedroom. They can't list it for that because the den doesn't have a closet. You'll have to buy an armoire, that's all. Ree said it's a nice place and the rent should be cheaper than getting a real two bedroom, so it might work for you."

And it wasn't in the middle of a smelly apartment building. They were walking into one of the quieter neighborhoods in the city, but they weren't more than a half mile from the restaurant. It might be a perfect setup for Shaw and Craw, once Carley and Taylor figured out whether or not they were working for the enemy and were therefore approved to stay, that is.

The neighborhood was empty at this time of day. Everyone was at work or school, so the houses were unoccupied. There wouldn't be a better time to confront Shaw and Craw with few witnesses or other people who might get hurt.

"I went looking for unusual patterns," Taylor said, abruptly cutting into the middle of Nevada's explanation. "Places where you used to live had a number of very odd deaths where people were gutted and thrown out of a car. You two weren't even here a day before a murder like that happened here, were you?"

Everyone had stopped walking, and Taylor watched as Shaw and Craw both took two steps back so they were next to each other, facing Nevada and Taylor. Shaw was slightly huddled behind Craw, like always, but Taylor wasn't able to let his guard down because of that.

"Antony was a Reyes, but he was a bad egg. The overall loss to the family was only in political clout. The problem is, he knew who is trying to disrupt this city, and I needed to talk to him. Getting answers from a dead body is much more difficult, which I think was the real point."

Taylor waited, carefully watching both brothers for any twitch that might signal an attack. They didn't move, instead continuing to watch Nevada and Taylor as if they were the ones expecting to be attacked.

"Are you hit men for hire?" Taylor added after the moment stretched on for a bit too long. They didn't answer.

"What Taylor isn't telling you is you haven't yet done anything that would get you kicked out of the city," Nevada said. "We're legitimately going apartment hunting with you, and Rosto is still eager to hire you both."

There was just the tiniest relaxation in Craw's shoulders at Nevada's words, enough to let Taylor know the softer approach might be the right track.

Taylor shrugged as if to say he didn't care, which he honestly didn't. He wasn't after a confession to their myriad crimes. "You're not the first killers to want to settle here, and I doubt you'll be the last. If you can obey the laws of the city, there's no reason to deny you the same chance we give everyone else that petitions the lord for residency. We have two conditions in your case. One, no more killing in this city. Two, you tell us who hired you to kill Antony."

Taylor waited a beat to let that sink in, but when they continued to stand frozen, he asked again. "Who hired you?"

Craw finally moved, but only to drop a gentle hand on Shaw's arm. "A man in a fancy suit, kind of like the guy who was holding a gun on us in the graveyard."

Taylor waited another second to see if Craw had anything more to say, but he had apparently said all he was willing to. Carley would have arrested them both on the spot for the confession—Taylor knew that—and he also knew Carley's entire intent would be to coerce the full story out of them. Shaw and Craw might know more about the coup, or have some hidden tidbits about the man who hired them, something that could help Taylor, and yet, Nevada's gentler approach was working so much better. Pushing wouldn't give Taylor anything; it would likely only make them more defensive. Gaining their trust, and proving through his words and actions that Taylor trusted them in turn, would be slower, but much more effective in the end. Taylor turned toward Nevada. He didn't quite give Shaw and Craw his back, but it was enough to show them he didn't consider them a threat.

"How did Ree find out about this place anyway?" Taylor asked Nevada as they both returned to walking down the street.

Nevada eyed Taylor as if to say he wasn't satisfied with the answer Craw had given, but he played along anyway. "She's looking to move out of her mother's house and had a tour of this place a few days ago. It's a little too far from the new restaurant where she's transferring to work. She's got a car, but felt silly having such a long commute when she could just find somewhere closer." Most importantly, Ree had already vetted whether the homeowner would be comfortable renting to Ge-Mis.

The soft pad of footsteps behind Taylor told him Craw and Shaw were still with them. It wasn't long before they reached the house in question, and a simple stone-paved walkway led them around the side of the house to a private entrance. A woman was waiting there, and she smiled when she saw them before opening the door for them to go inside.

The place was as advertised. One bedroom, but the den had windows and a door with a lock on it. The one bathroom was accessible to the entire apartment, and it had a double sink. Even the kitchen looked clean and modern.

"Laundry is through here," the homeowner said. She went to a door at the very back of the apartment and pulled it open. The door had a big lock on the inside. It led into a short hallway with only a washer and dryer inside. On the other end was another heavy door. "That leads to my house," she said. "We share the laundry, so don't be leaving your things in here."

They returned to the main room, and Taylor watched Craw take another look around the space. "It's ideal." It was also unfurnished, which would be expensive to fix, although with two decent salaries from the restaurant they would be able to afford it.

"First two months' rent due now and a five-hundred-dollar security deposit," the homeowner said. Craw's face fell immediately, and Taylor could guess why. Money didn't grow on trees, and they had been sleeping in alleys the last few nights rather than renting a room in a hotel.

"Do you take fingerprints?" Taylor asked.

The woman's face brightened, and she nodded before bustling off to the front door and the bag she had left there when they walked in.

"You can't," Craw gasped.

Taylor held out his finger when the woman returned, ignoring Craw for the moment. He pressed it to the scanner and watched as the homeowner input the correct amount. He scanned his finger again and typed his passcode, and then it was done.

"No one is homeless in Kensey," Taylor said firmly. "Besides, you'll pay the lord back with your taxes. This isn't charity; it's practicality." And it ensured they felt at least a little indebted to Taylor. Maybe next time he asked them who hired them, he would get a better answer. "We'll leave you to work out the final details and sign the contract." He reached out to take Nevada's hand, and they headed toward the door.

"I have to go get ready for work," Nevada said sadly once they were outside. He looked over his shoulder at the house and smiled at him. "That was really nice of you."

Taylor smiled back. "No, it wasn't. Crime goes down when everyone has a safe place to sleep at night, and now I know exactly where those two will be. It's much easier to keep track of them this way."

"If you say so," Nevada replied, and the cheerful tone of his voice said he wasn't buying it.

Taylor let it go, mostly because Nevada wasn't exactly wrong. "I wish I could walk you home, but I have to get to work too."

Nevada shrugged, but his smile dimmed a bit. "It's okay. You can pick me up after work instead."

"Deal," Taylor replied. He leaned forward to press a kiss to the tip of Nevada's nose and grinned when Nevada scrunched it unhappily.

Nevada pushed forward to take a proper kiss, and when they were done, all Taylor wanted to do was helplessly follow Nevada home to do some more wickedly wonderful things together. The twist to Nevada's lips said he wanted the same thing, but he still pulled away.

"Work," Nevada said firmly. "You're picking me up afterward," he added, and the promise of continuing later was in every syllable.

"Right," Taylor ground out, his voice rough. He took a step back to remove temptation. "Have a good day."

"I will." Nevada turned and walked off down the street. He only got a few houses away before LeeAnne joined him, so at least Taylor didn't have to worry about Nevada for the rest of the afternoon. Taylor took a deep breath and forced himself to turn around and start walking in the other direction.

"You've got it bad," Drew said as he joined Taylor. He had been discreetly tailing them with LeeAnne all morning. There was cat hair all over Drew's pants, from his knees down, and Taylor couldn't help the snicker that escaped. "I think you've got it worse. Hex apparently really likes you."

"Likes to torture me is more like it," Drew replied with a low rumbling growl. "Can I eat him?"

Taylor didn't bother answering that. They kept walking, and it wasn't long before they stepped onto the street leading to the pack house, and farther along, to the mansion.

"That's the second time someone's implicated Carley as the culprit," Drew said softly, but pointedly. No doubt he and LeeAnne had been within earshot of that part of the conversation with Craw.

"I know, and it's bothering me too." Taylor shook his head. "It just doesn't make sense that Carley would be the culprit."

"It does to me. Just because the man changed your diapers doesn't mean he won't try to kill you now." Drew reached out and rested a comforting hand on Taylor's shoulder. "I know he's basically been your father figure your entire life, but you have to look at this without any sentiment."

"It's not that," Taylor replied, although he had to admit to himself that part of it could be. "Think about it.

Carley is the third most powerful person in this city. He has unprecedented access to me and to Gramps; he wouldn't need all this rigmarole to take over. Carley's had more than enough opportunity to kill me and Gramps, and it would be easy for him to take over from there. None of my cousins have the acumen to compete with him for control, and he knows it."

Drew sighed and let out a nod. "Okay, that makes sense. Why do you think two of the witnesses have pointed to him, then?"

"Probably for the same reason they tried to implicate Rosto a few weeks ago." It was the best answer Taylor could come up with, and he hoped it was right. "Sow a little distrust and we start to break down. Allows them to get a wedge in."

"Bastards. We need to catch them."

Taylor nodded. "We're working on it. Until then, we all need to keep watching our backs."

They walked the last few blocks in silence. Drew turned into the house when they reached it, likely ready to go another round with Hex, and Taylor continued up the hill to the mansion. He let himself inside and headed down into the maze. This time he went to his own office where a datapad was waiting for him. He logged in and saw a lengthy list of paperwork he needed to handle. It took about two hours to go through each document and either sign it or send it back for revisions. Taylor looked at the clock when he was done and sighed. Two hours before his lunch meeting with the finance committee, which left him enough time to start digging.

He was supposed to think Carley was the one orchestrating the coup, but there was an easy way to know it wasn't him. The two idiots on the roof had said they had seen a man in a suit driving the car. If Taylor could find out where Carley really was during that timeframe, he would have enough proof to rule him out.

Taylor logged into the mansion's surveillance system through his account as the heir to the throne. Carley might have access to almost everything, but Taylor had just a bit more. If Carley had altered any surveillance logs, Taylor's additional access would tell him.

Oliver's final report stated Antony's body had been lying in the parking lot for approximately six hours when they found him at 10:00 a.m., which meant the car had driven by overhead at about 4:00 a.m. That was about the time Taylor had finally given up searching and headed first to the pack house to debrief, and then eventually to Nevada's, but Carley hadn't stopped. He had been on his phone with Taylor off and on the whole night, which didn't place him in the mansion, but said he was working. Taylor hooked into the surveillance system the evening before, when he was waiting outside Café Spice and had received the first call from Carley, who should have been in the mansion at the time.

It didn't take long to ID him walking out of his office toward the computer lab around midnight. He left around 2:00 a.m. for a bathroom run and returned to his office from there. And then, at 3:30 a.m., he headed up the stairs and out of the mansion.

Taylor frowned and called up the metadata for that section of film. He scrolled through the code and had to admit he was impressed. There wasn't a single blip or inconsistent mark that he could identify. Of course, that could be because there wasn't anything to see, but Taylor knew Carley. If Carley had been the one behind all of this, he would have altered the data to show he was there the entire time.

The hacker had done a really good job, but recoding at the level of security Taylor had access to required DNA. The bite of the scanner was a momentary annoyance before the original information came up on the screen.

The video flickered, and then the date time stamp changed to three weeks earlier, which Taylor guessed was the last time Carley was wearing a blue shirt. Three thirty on the real tape showed Carley still in his office. He stayed there until eight, at which point the camera caught him heading rapidly upstairs with his phone pressed to his ear. He would call Taylor a little over an hour later.

Taylor leaned back in his chair and frowned at the frozen image of Carley heading up the stairs. The rest of the metadata was clean, which meant Carley was being set up. Taylor knew why it was happening, but he didn't know by whom. It wasn't as if the hacker had left a signature...or maybe they had, of a sort. He scrolled back up to the start of the coding changes, where the system had been told to run the old video footage, and dug into the files stored in the mansion servers rather than the individual cameras' hard drives. If he could find the same style of coding elsewhere, perhaps attached to a legitimate project assignment, he might be able to find a name.

A few clicks had that search running automatically. There was far too much data to search by hand. Which reminded Taylor of another quick search he wanted to set up to run while he was in his meeting. A glance at the clock said he still had twenty minutes, so Taylor pulled up city biometric data for the day of Antony's death and started looking for the two drugged idiots that had told him a car, flying by at speed overhead, had been driven by a man in a suit. They had been in place for the body drop, but at their level of inebriation, Taylor had doubts about every part of their story except the 'woooo, splat' and the 'woooo, crack' statements.

Taylor should have done this search that day, but he had been distracted by funeral preparations. Better late than never though. If he could identify the idiots, he might be able to figure out who paid them to say something they had likely never seen.

Once that second search was set to run while he was away, Taylor stood and stretched, letting his back pop after sitting still for so long. He had barely enough time to run upstairs and tell Gramps what he had found before he had to go sit through that meeting.

Taylor left his office and headed upstairs, winding his way back through the maze until he arrived in one of the main hallways of the mansion. The fastest way to Gramps's office was through the large atrium ahead, so Taylor cut down that way, hoping he didn't run into anyone who would delay him. He couldn't be late to the meeting. Except, he could hear yelling as some sort of ruckus started up ahead. That wouldn't do. The mansion was the seat of government for Kensey, and as such, needed to be treated with respect. Arguments were supposed to be kept to the courtrooms, not the public hallways. He hurried forward but stopped short in the entrance.

"What is going on here?" Taylor yelled over the noise. Carley was in handcuffs, his arms wrenched tight behind his back with two armored guards holding him between them. The sight hit Taylor's stomach heavy like a rock had settled down there. Carley was the man who had changed his diapers, rocked him back to sleep when he had nightmares, let him dig up the garden just because Taylor wanted to, and cleaned up his scrapes and his tears whenever he got in a fight with someone who was being mean to him. Taylor might not know who his blood father was, but he knew who had raised him alongside Gramps, and there was no way he was going to let this happen.

Taylor strode forward into the sudden silence at his words, heading straight for Carley.

"Taylor." Gramps never had to yell. His voice always penetrated, even in a completely quiet room, and Taylor found his feet coming to a stop after only a few steps.

"Yes, Taylor," Uncle Jeff added. He walked around from behind Carley, where it looked like he had previously been leading the guards outside, and stopped in the middle of the atrium where everyone could see him. "We have caught the traitor who killed Antony. Surely that must make you happy?"

"Carley's not a traitor," Taylor said, and it was only thanks to Gramps's stern eye that he kept his tone polite.

Uncle Jeff scoffed. "You yourself interviewed two eye witnesses who put him at the scene of Antony's murder. I viewed the surveillance tapes that show him leaving the mansion with just enough time to commit the attack. I arrested him myself."

Taylor opened his mouth, a protest and the truth ready to spill out, when he caught the slightest shake of Carley's head. No, Carley was telling Taylor, and Taylor wanted desperately to shout "Why?" Instead, he closed his mouth and studied Uncle Jeff.

Uncle Jeff was Gramps's sister's oldest son, and he shared the blond hair and lean build of all Reyes stock. He was born a few years before Taylor's mother, and had Taylor not been chosen as heir, he would have been next in line. Antony was Jeff's younger sister's middle child, and their relationship had been fairly close. Everything about Uncle Jeff fit the profile Gramps and Carley had constructed, and Taylor knew he had been high on the suspect list. He had just made number one as far as Taylor was concerned.

It wasn't only that he fit the profile, of course. The confident, almost arrogant way he was standing—as if he had won the game they were playing—set Taylor's teeth on edge.

"This is a serious charge," Gramps finally said when Jeff's explanation hung in the room for too long.

Taylor looked around and saw what Carley and Gramps must already have. Antony's parents were there, and they looked convinced of Uncle Jeff's story. Uncle Stephen, Gramps's younger brother, didn't look as certain, but two of his grandsons standing nearby did. Uncle Jeff had supporters in the room, people who would automatically concur with Uncle Jeff's claims. If Taylor or Gramps tried to discount Uncle Jeff now, surrounded by people almost certain of Carley's guilt, Gramps wouldn't have to worry about a simple coup; he would have to worry about the entire Reyes family banding together against him. The city of Kensey would be destroyed in the resulting civil war. The fighting wouldn't remain quiet— no more poisoning attempts or backroom maneuvering. Reyes would fight against Reyes in the streets with actual guns, each faction trying to get their chosen leader to the top, and Kensey would suffer in the crossfire.

"However," Gramps continued, "all you bring before me is supposition. Two of the witnesses were high on drugs, I believe, and it is entirely possible Mr. Lensington was simply going home after spending all night and most of the morning fruitlessly searching for Antony, who we knew was missing."

Uncle Stephen put restraining hands on both his grandsons' shoulders, so Taylor knew at least some people were hearing what Gramps was saying. Antony's parents looked murderous, furious expressions darkening their faces. Uncle Jeff still looked confident, but Taylor thought perhaps a touch of his arrogance had faded. Certainly, Taylor's own heart had resumed beating in his chest, and the stone in his stomach was now a pebble instead.

"At the same time, we cannot allow such charges to go uninvestigated. Guards." Gramps turned to the two men holding Carley in place. "I believe Mr. Lensington will enjoy a stint of house arrest. Please escort him to his home, and ensure the biometrics on the house are set properly?"

Both guards nodded politely before turning and leading Carley out of the room. It was better than being dragged, which had been what was happening when Taylor first entered the atrium, but seeing Carley go wrenched something inside Taylor's chest.

Gramps walked over to Taylor next, and he placed a gentle hand on Taylor's arm. Taylor got the message: Gramps had this in hand. "I believe you have a finance meeting you're about to be late for?" he said to Taylor.

Taylor let out a heavy breath of air through his nose. As if he could concentrate on something as boring as finances right now. Gramps's hand tightened slightly, losing the gentle touch and turning toward chiding. Again, Taylor got the unspoken message: it didn't matter whether the sky was falling; he still had a city to run, and he had better buck up and do it.

"I was just heading there when I heard a ruckus," Taylor replied, trying to make his voice sound easy and unworried. He wasn't sure it worked, but Gramps's hand loosened with approval. "I'll see you for dinner?"

Gramps nodded. "Yes. We should, hopefully, have this misunderstanding wrapped up by then. I look forward to it."

Taylor nodded to Gramps before continuing on his way toward the stairs that led up to the meeting rooms. As

Taylor turned, he caught Uncle Jeff impatiently shifting his weight, but then Gramps walked up to Uncle Jeff, who quickly started talking at Gramps. Taylor didn't stick around to see how it would go. He had a city to run, and right now, more than ever, it was time to prove his competence by not only being on time for the meeting, but knowing what he was doing. Every ally he could gain that way was one fewer voice supporting Uncle Jeff. Taylor didn't need Gramps's hand on his arm to understand that one.

Chapter Seven

"So then Rosto overheard they would be sleeping on the floor. He gave them an advance on their first paychecks and is going with them tomorrow morning to pick out beds, a couch, and a kitchen table set." Nevada paused to eat some of the pasta still on his plate. Taylor wasn't eating, just swirling his food around his plate with his fork, but he was enjoying watching Nevada's animated face. He seemed so happy with life, and that made Taylor happy until he remembered Carley wasn't sitting with them tonight and that put a damper on things.

"Your new staff appear to be settling in well," Gramps said while Nevada chewed. "They'll have to come present themselves officially at the next court session. Just make sure they don't bring a cat as a bribe." That got the laugh Gramps was going for, and Princess Pea let out a well-timed snort from where she was lounging underneath Nevada's chair.

"Rosto explained the process to them. I'm sure they'll come up with something." Nevada shrugged, acting nonchalant, but Taylor knew better. Nevada would help

Shaw and Craw come up with a suitable bribe if he had to. They really had become friends. Taylor would have been jealous, except Nevada had chosen to sit next to him at the dinner table for what he knew would be a difficult evening, rather than hanging out with his friends for the night.

The reason for the difficult evening slammed his fork down onto the table and leaned forward in his seat. "Don't we have more important things to discuss right now, like the traitor?" Uncle Jeff snarled. He had invited himself over, ostensibly because Carley usually joined them, and Uncle Jeff thought he would be taking Carley's security job. What Uncle Jeff didn't understand was Carley didn't join them for dinner because he was the chief of security and practically ran the city, but because he was family.

"We do not discuss work at the dinner table," Gramps replied easily with only a slight chiding note in his voice. He turned to face Uncle Jeff. "I hear your oldest, Samantha, is turning into a fine lawyer."

Taylor tuned them out, happy to focus all of his attention on Nevada, who looked like he was three seconds away from licking his plate clean. Except, Nevada's eyes flicked from Uncle Jeff to Taylor, and the quizzical look in them told Taylor Nevada wasn't missing any of the nuances of this particular meal.

Later, Taylor mouthed before finally eating some of his food. It tasted like pasta and white sauce, heavy with cheese and earthy mushrooms, and it was delicious, but it took a few tries before he could actually force his throat to swallow. Taylor didn't know if Nevada was taking pity on him, or simply wanted more, but his fork stole over onto Taylor's plate and pushed half of what remained over onto his own plate. Another agonizing ten minutes passed before Gramps finally stood.

"We'll have coffee in the sitting room," Gramps told one of the waiting servants, who nodded politely before hurrying off. Gramps led the way out of the dining room and down the hall, Uncle Jeff tight on his heels. Taylor held back with Nevada, and once he was certain they were out of earshot, he leaned in close and began to explain.

"I know it wasn't Carley because I found the original metadata," Taylor finished. "But how do I prove that when Uncle Jeff is aiming to take over? It'll cause a civil war."

Nevada shook his head in answer. "Go have coffee. Now that we know who it is, we can watch him, but for the moment we continue acting as if everything is normal." He reached out and ran his fingers over one of Taylor's pointed ears, his nails digging in perfectly at the joint. Taylor dropped his head onto Nevada's chest, and he let the comfort of the intimate touch flow through him.

It had been a shitty day, although it had started well and was ending well. Funny that the parts he had liked had been the time spent with Nevada. Well, maybe funny wasn't the right word. Relieving, maybe? Taylor didn't know, and with Nevada's fingers combing through his hair and hitting his ears just right, Taylor couldn't really come up with a coherent thought anyway.

"If you two are done?" Gramps's voice cut through Taylor like a hot knife through butter. He reluctantly pulled away from Nevada, but clasped his hand as they walked together into the sitting room. "The coffee's probably cold now," Gramps said as they settled into the loveseat together.

"Now, now," Uncle Jeff cut in, his voice trying to be soothing, but there was a condescending note to it that had Taylor gritting his teeth. "I remember when I first met my wife. Every stolen moment we could get together was extremely important."

Gramps frowned at him. "I seem to remember finding you both in darkened corners of the mansion doing something inappropriate at least twice."

Uncle Jeff didn't reply to that, although Taylor was gratified to see a slight blush staining his cheeks. Gramps was reminding Jeff that he wasn't so different than Taylor; after all, human was still human. Just because Taylor wasn't all human didn't mean he wasn't still similar to Uncle Jeff and the rest of the Reyes family.

Taylor leaned forward so he could reach the table where coffee and dessert was set out and picked up the teapot instead. There were some canine Ge-Mis that couldn't handle coffee; Taylor wasn't one of them, but he preferred tea at the end of the day, as did Nevada. He poured them both cups, which were still steaming and perfectly hot, and handed one to Nevada.

"How was the finance meeting this afternoon?" Gramps asked Taylor, who ignored Uncle Jeff opening his mouth, likely to complain they weren't starting with his agenda.

"They're not happy about the new shopping center we're looking to build. Said the money would be better spent resurfacing the sidewalks and parking lots in the Remington neighborhood." Taylor took a sip of tea and tried not to wince. It was still a little too hot, but he didn't think he had burned his tongue. "I reminded them that the funds for the sidewalks had already been allotted and a construction crew hired to start that work in the spring. The shopping center was a new project to help support the three new apartment complexes going up nearby."

"Did they approve it?" Gramps asked.

Taylor nodded and blew on his tea. "Tentative approval with an official vote in session next week."

"Excellent job—"

"What about the traitor!" Uncle Jeff exclaimed, cutting Gramps off midsentence.

Gramps let out a slow, heavy breath of air as if he were taking a moment to steel his patience. "I need a motive before I'm willing to believe someone as loyal as Carley Lensington has suddenly turned traitor."

Uncle Jeff scoffed. "To take over the city, of course. To rule Kensey."

This time both Taylor and Gramps shook their heads in denial, but Taylor let Gramps continue explaining. "Carley could have taken over the city any time in the last twenty years. He was here when I was at my most vulnerable after losing my daughter; he has been my second while Taylor was growing up, and now he continues to educate Taylor to someday rule. It would have been simple for him to take over without any need for subterfuge or to use and abuse traitors like Antony Reyes."

"Antony was a traitor?" Uncle Jeff asked, but the amount of disbelief in his voice said he didn't believe it for a second.

"We found a suspiciously large amount of money exchanging hands with Antony acting as the middleman. The money would go into a secret bank account of which Antony was the executor and would then be sent to people we suspect were part of this coup attempt. Most of the money trail is lost in Morse, but we did identify payments to a certain group of hyenas."

That was actually how they had found Antony's secret account: backtracking the money sent to the hyenas. Carley had done most of the work, but Taylor had looked it over and didn't remember seeing anything inaccurate.

"Antony could have been...buying drugs?" Uncle Jeff's retort was weak, and he knew it. He stared into his coffee cup for a long moment before looking up at Gramps again. "Why would Antony turn traitor? He was such a good kid with a bright future ahead of him."

Taylor could answer that. "He hated Ge-Mis. Seeing me named heir likely tipped him over the edge. Whoever was organizing the coup took advantage of his prejudice, and when they found out we were looking for Antony, they had him silenced." Taylor was looking at Uncle Jeff closely as he said the last bit and was surprised when Uncle Jeff only slowly shook his head in sad disbelief. There wasn't a hint of smugness, or of his trying to school his face. Either he was an amazing actor—which Taylor didn't think was true or he would have hidden his attitude better when he arrested Carley—or he wasn't actually the traitor.

Gramps must have seen the same thing. "Who alerted you to the discrepancy in the surveillance footage?"

"What?" Uncle Jeff gasped. "No, I'm not being used like Antony."

"Your sister is distraught over her son's death. You are, too, and I have no doubt you are looking to solve the murder and bring peace back to you both." Gramps's voice was gentle but firm. "I'm sorry to say that it would have been easy for someone to slip a bug in your ear."

"But the footage showed Carley leaving at exactly the right time..."

"Altered," Taylor said when Uncle Jeff trailed off. "The metadata shows a hacker got in and replaced the footage with something from three weeks earlier."

"Who told you?" Gramps was still being gentle, but forceful. They needed this information, and the sooner they had it, the sooner they could start working to free Carley and prevent the civil war.

Uncle Jeff was slumped in his seat, his coffee mug hanging precariously from one limp hand, but as Taylor watched, he came to some sort of resolution because he sat up again, and some of his swagger came back.

"Stephen," he said softly. "It was Stephen, but you're not going to get to him so easily."

Gramps harrumphed, but it was mostly for show. Uncle Jeff was right. After Gramps, Carley, and Taylor, Uncle Stephen held the most power in Kensey. He wouldn't have ever seen the throne, not with Taylor and even Uncle Jeff in the way, but removing Carley and turning Uncle Jeff into the antagonist would clear the way for him to step forward and take it all once the dust finally settled again. Uncle Stephen's ingenious plan would have worked, and the thought had Taylor repressing an angry snarl. He was squeezing Nevada's hand too tightly in an attempt to contain himself, but Nevada was squeezing back and his attention was entirely focused on Uncle Jeff and Gramps.

"I have recently learned I have been remiss," Gramps began slowly, temporarily ignoring the revelation Uncle Jeff had just dropped. "I have relied almost completely on citizens dwelling in my city for understanding on how the city works. They have done an excellent job, but they are only citizens. They are not Reyeses. Carley will get his job back, but he mentioned he could use a second-in-command to help with much of his work. I was thinking I might like to fill it with family, and, Jeff, if you're interested, I would like to hire you."

Start with the stick, end with the carrot. Taylor had learned that trick at Gramps's knee when he was little, but he had never seen it used with quite so much skill. If Uncle Jeff accepted, he was theirs.

Uncle Jeff let out a hard laugh. "Of course, I want it. It's another way Stephen was able to convince me to help. Remove Carley Lensington and, he said, the job would be mine."

"The position I can give you would be working under Carley, but I assure you it is one of vital importance. Come, let's go to my office and iron out the details."

Maybe Uncle Jeff was capable of doing the work, although if that were true Gramps would have hired him already. Uncle Jeff was one of those people who thought his last name and his money meant he should be given handouts for everything. Taylor doubted he had ever worked a day in his life or would be capable of handling the long hours and stress of Carley's position. Luckily, Carley would know how to make Uncle Jeff feel like he was important without letting him have any real responsibility. Maybe, just maybe, Carley would be able to teach Uncle Jeff what an honest day's work actually looked like, and Uncle Jeff would turn around. Taylor had doubts, but, thankfully, that was Gramps's problem to solve.

"Taylor, will you be sleeping in the mansion tonight?" Gramps asked, pausing in the doorway in front of Uncle Jeff.

Taylor shook his head. "I'm at Nevada's tonight. He has to feed his ankle biters." That got him a shove in the arm, but it made Nevada smile wryly, so it was a win as far as Taylor was concerned. Gramps nodded, and Taylor knew he had heard the unspoken message. Taylor would be at Nevada's to protect him until the coup attempt was ended.

Gramps was waiting, so Taylor gave Nevada's hand one last squeeze before standing and walking over to give Gramps a hug good night. Once Gramps and Uncle Jeff left, Taylor reached out and took Nevada's hand in his, and they walked together out of the mansion and back down the hill to Nevada's apartment.

Chapter Eight

"Is this month's court session still going to happen?" Nevada asked at breakfast the next morning. Taylor ran the brush through his tail one last time before returning it to the bathroom counter and heading out into the kitchen.

Nevada was talking about the monthly session where supplicants of all kinds came to speak with Gramps about issues they were having. Often it was petty stuff, for which Gramps happily took a bribe to see about fixing, and newcomers to the city came to present themselves and ask for permission to stay, but sometimes serious matters were brought up. Now that Taylor was thinking about it, if Uncle Stephen were interested in making even more of a public display than arresting Carley in the mansion atrium, using the court session would be ideal. He would have to mention it to Gramps to see what might be done to prepare for that.

"It's in two days," Taylor answered after double-checking the calendar on his phone. "Why?"

Nevada shrugged. "I'm wondering whether Shaw and Craw should declare themselves more openly. Get the fact that we know about them into view, so they can stop being used as pawns to kill for someone else."

That wasn't a bad idea. Taylor told Nevada, but another stray thought flittered by at the same time. Shaw and Craw had been brought to the city to kill Antony, after which they should have been paid for their services. Instead, they had been sleeping in alleys and had needed Taylor and Rosto's help to get their apartment situated. Where had the money gone?

That was another search he could run.

It would be so much easier if he could call Carley, and Taylor's fingers twitched toward the cell phone in his pocket before he remembered Carley's situation. Uncle Stephen had been very effective at stymying Taylor's ability to get things done quickly; he was so used to calling Carley, who would get the searches started on the computer before Taylor arrived in the maze. Instead, Taylor would have to do it himself, and he would need to be in the mansion to do it, which meant he would need to leave Nevada. If Uncle Stephen were really looking to destroy Taylor, going after Nevada would be the most effective way. It didn't matter that the hyenas had tried and failed to take him out not too long ago; Taylor knew he still needed to be careful.

He shot off a quick text to LeeAnne and got a response a moment later. She and Drew would walk Nevada to work and keep an eye out for him until Taylor could pick him up that night. With one worry taken care of, Taylor finally tucked into his bowl of cereal.

"Have a good day at work," Nevada said once they had finished eating. He was rinsing their bowls in the sink since he didn't need to head out for at least another hour, but he tilted his chin up in silent demand.

Taylor couldn't refuse and found his feet moving toward Nevada almost before his brain processed the particular angle to Nevada's neck and the way his eyes slid half closed as Taylor bent down. Lips touched and breath mingled, and all Taylor wanted to do was sink into Nevada and forget the rest of the world existed. Except he couldn't and that twinge of responsibility forced him to slowly pull away. He ran his fingers over the curve of Nevada's soft ear before taking a step backward.

"I'll see you tonight," he said softly, and then wrenched himself around and walked to the door.

The trip to the manor was a familiar one. Taylor kept an eye on his surroundings, but his heart was back at Nevada's apartment and his brain was already parsing through all the data he would have to go through as soon as he got to a computer. It wasn't long before he reached the maze and the computer, and he pushed everything else away to sink into research.

*

Taylor blinked, then blinked again. He slowly lifted his head from where it had been resting on his folded arms. When had he fallen asleep? How, was actually the better question. Taylor remembered the holo images floating around him and the realization that Shaw and Craw really were broke, which meant they had never been paid. Taylor remembered sitting back in his chair, wondering at that, because any good assassin would get at least some money up front before committing to anything, and yet Antony was still dead. Taylor's last thought had been whether Shaw and Craw had actually been the ones who killed Antony. And now he was waking up…

Taylor shot to his feet and looked around, adrenaline burning off the last of whatever had kept him so sluggish for the last few moments. He wasn't in the computer lab. No, he was in some sort of small closet with only the chair he had been sitting in and the table he had been leaning on as decorations. There was a door across the room with bars where a small window ought to be and a small cat flap at the bottom, likely where he would get delivered food.

There was no doubt in Taylor's mind that the door was locked, but he still leapt over the table to grip the knob. He put his back into it, yanking with all his strength, and the hinges groaned, but he was part wolf, not part bear, and the metal held.

He had to get out of here. Had to. He couldn't stay in a cage, and he couldn't be captured right now. He had to be there for Gramps, for Carley, and for…Nevada! What if they had gotten Nevada too! Taylor yanked at the doorknob again. The entire door rattled in its frame, but the lock held.

"I'm sorry."

Taylor growled at the sudden noise and jumped away from the door, his hands out in front of his face with his fingers curled into claws. It took a second for his heartbeat to slow and the roaring in his brain to subside enough he could hear the repeated "I'm sorry" filter through the barred window.

He didn't recognize the voice, but when first a pointed black ear and then the familiar face of Shaw came into view in the window, Taylor knew why. He didn't think he had ever heard Shaw talk before; he was usually hiding behind Craw.

"Let me out. Now!"

Shaw flinched backward but then squared his shoulders and returned to the window. "I have to tell you things, now, before it's too late."

"I already know you didn't kill Antony. You weren't paid for it," Taylor cut in. "Let me out so I can let everyone else know before my grandfather changes his mind and has you arrested."

Shaw shook his head. "We were promised a job if we traveled to Kensey, yes, but your cousin was already dead by the time we arrived. That's not what I have to tell you. I need to tell you about how we're supposed to kill you, because you're the one we were hired to kill, sir."

Taylor's heart stuttered in his chest. "What about Nevada? Where's Nevada?" His voice was choked out at barely more than a whisper, but Shaw heard him.

This time Shaw smiled, and there was a mischievous twist to his lips that was totally incongruous to Taylor snarling at him or the gravity of the situation. "We tried to grab him, too, but he has too many guard dogs surrounding him all the time. At least—" He paused and his grin grew wider. "—that's what we told our employer."

Taylor's knees went limp, and he sagged against the table in relief. "So Nevada's okay," he breathed out.

Shaw nodded. "He's… We've never had friends, me and Craw. We always had to be so careful not to get found out, so we kept to ourselves. But Nevada knew we were murderers, and he wanted to be friends, anyway."

Taylor knew that particular tone of voice, having heard the combination of exasperation and love in his own voice when he was first figuring out what made Nevada tick. It made him smile, even with the locked door between them.

"You need to let me out before Nevada gets worried," Taylor said, trying to work with Shaw's emotions. Taylor would do anything—absolutely anything—to get out of his cage and return to combating Uncle Stephen before something worse than getting kidnapped from the mansion happened to his family.

"It's too late for that." Shaw shook his head. "The drugs we gave you knocked you out for a full day." Taylor's stomach dropped at the news. "In exactly eight hours, we're supposed to introduce ourselves at this month's court session by dumping your body in the room and declaring a new Kensey heir. That's what we were hired to do, and that's what we're going to do."

There was so much to unpack here that Taylor's head was spinning over all of it. He sat on the tabletop, so he could watch Shaw in the window while he tried to figure it all out.

First was the fact that he was here rather than in the computer lab down in the maze, which was behind password-protected doors. Only someone with access could get down there, and only someone familiar with the maze would know where Taylor's office was. Shaw and Craw wouldn't have been able to grab him without help, and getting him out of the mansion past the guards covering every door meant multiple traitors were involved.

Then came the question about Shaw, primarily whether Taylor could trust him. Taylor wanted to. Something about the earnest look on Shaw's face, the way he had called Taylor "sir," and the way he spoke about Nevada all worked to convince Taylor that Shaw was on the level. Yet, he was an assassin for hire. Could Taylor really afford to trust him?

Could Taylor afford not to trust him?

"I assume since I'm alive right now, you have a different plan in mind?" Taylor slid off the desk and stepped back up to the window, where he curled his hands around the bars. He could see and smell Shaw clearly now; hopefully, he would notice a twitch or a spike of the sour smell of anxiety if Shaw was lying.

Shaw nodded. "We had to grab you. There were too many people involved with that operation for us to not follow through. Later, I'll make sure you know every single person involved, but for right now, we need to talk about tonight. Everyone will be in the court session. Lord Reyes, Nevada, even Stephen Reyes, because we can't declare him the new heir if he isn't present."

"And I have to be there," Taylor added, starting to catch on.

"Exactly." Shaw grinned shyly at him. "But that doesn't mean you have to come alone."

"Tell me," Taylor said. The lock clicked and the door swung open. Taylor stepped out into freedom, and Shaw started talking.

Chapter Nine

Taylor had thought he knew every inch of the Reyes manor. He had explored every room as a child trying to find somewhere to hide: from bullies, from expectations, and when he wanted just to flop out in a warm patch of sun where no one would bother him for a while. He had never explored behind the ceiling tiles, and after this was over, Taylor was going to make certain no one else ever had the opportunity to do what Shaw and Craw had shown him how to do. How Shaw and Craw had figured out there was enough crawl space over the ceiling tiles for a person to comfortably lay was another issue.

A crack in one of the tiles—a rather conveniently placed crack, which was yet another issue Taylor was cataloguing for later—allowed him to see most of the room and the dais where Gramps and Taylor usually sat. Nevada and Gramps were there now, as was Uncle Jeff, who was standing behind Gramps where Carley usually stood. Uncle Stephen was leaning against the door that led back into the private areas of the manor, effectively cutting off Gramps's escape route.

It all felt so staged, but it shouldn't have. Gramps and Nevada weren't supposed to know what was about to happen. Nevada looked worried. He was chewing on his lower lip, and the tip of his tail was twitching. Gramps looked completely normal, as if this were just another court session. Uncle Jeff looked wide-eyed and overwhelmed, and Taylor didn't doubt he was regretting his sudden rise in responsibility. Either Uncle Jeff would handle it, or he would quietly step down. He wasn't the problem here. No, the problem was Uncle Stephen, who had never before attended a court session and who was looking a little too nonchalant leaning against the doorjamb.

There was a soft rustle to his right, up in the ceiling tiles where the rest of his wolves were hiding, and then a hiss from farther down to be quiet, and Taylor had to stifle his own snicker of laughter.

The courtroom was full of supplicants and courtiers, all hoping to catch Gramps's eye for whatever reason, but court hadn't started just yet. They were waiting as long as possible for Taylor to show, which wasn't going to happen until...there. The doors opened one last time, and in walked Shaw and Craw.

Nevada twitched, turning slightly in the direction of Shaw and Craw, but he didn't leave Gramps's side. Taylor frowned at that, wondering whether Nevada might actually have some idea of Taylor's whereabouts after all. Taylor's frown quickly turned into a fond smile, but he forced himself to pay attention as Gramps finally called for court to begin.

Taylor didn't know where on the list Shaw and Craw fell. He tried to wait patiently, but every minute he was stuck in the ceiling, watching Nevada also trying not to fidget, was agony. The fourth supplicant bowed and backed away, leaving behind a lovely picture of the Reyes mansion she had painted in return for some favor. Taylor was too far away to hear the particulars, but she was smiling, so she must have gotten what she wanted. Gramps wasn't smiling—not that he ever really did during court sessions, but he was much more stoic than usual. Taylor desperately wanted to alleviate his worry, but he had to wait for the right time. LeeAnne was with him in the ceiling along with all but two of his wolves, Drew and Mike, who were sneaking into position on the other side of the doorway Uncle Stephen was still holding up.

Uncle Stephen appeared totally unconcerned. His Reyes-blond hair was gelled back, and his face was completely stoic. He barely seemed interested in the proceedings, and he was looking at Shaw and Craw half as often as Nevada. If Taylor didn't know differently, he would have said Uncle Stephen didn't have a concern in the world, and maybe he didn't. Maybe he was so confident in how the evening was going to go, he wasn't worried about any of it. Taylor couldn't wait to prove him wrong.

The secretary with the ledger must have called Shaw and Craw because suddenly they were stepping forward to stand below the dais.

"Welcome to Kensey," Gramps said in his formal welcome statement. "I am glad to know you are settling in well. Have you any requests for this court?"

Taylor slid his fingers into the seam of the ceiling tile, ready to pull it out at the signal. Uncle Stephen finally moved a few steps closer to Gramps in the first evidence that he was more than a little interested in the proceedings.

"No requests," Craw said, and his voice somehow managed to reach the entire room. "We simply wanted to express our thanks for all your kindnesses. To that end, we have located your errant grandson."

That was Taylor's cue. Time to start the drama.

He yanked on the ceiling tile, expecting it to slide free, but it was heavier than it looked. Taylor let out a soft grunt and pushed up onto his knees, trying to get leverage in the tight space without alerting any of the guards or his enemies. He was officially late for his cue and noticed Shaw's hand creep up to grip the back of Craw's shirt.

If felt like a few minutes had passed, but Gramps was just opening his mouth to reply when Taylor finally had a grip on the tile. Then Uncle Stephen stepped forward.

"Yes, where is dear Taylor Reyes?" he asked softly, his voice somehow managing to quiet the room completely. Heads turned to watch as he strode forward to stand at an angle to Gramps so he could see both Gramps and Shaw and Craw at the same time.

"This is one of the most important meetings in Kensey, when the Reyes family deigns to interact with the regular public, and the heir—the heir!—has decided to skip it. Is he off howling at the moon? Too busy sniffing at sewer grates?" Uncle Stephen laughed coldly, but Taylor was gratified to note no one else in the room laughed with him.

The timing was too perfect to ignore. Taylor gave one last yank at the tile, and it finally slid free with a scrape that sounded impossibly loud to Taylor's ears, yet no one looked up. Everyone was so totally focused on Uncle Stephen standing on the dais, looking like a king next to Gramps's slightly stooped form. Taylor couldn't wait to take him down a peg or ten.

"Actually..." Taylor called out loud enough for the room to hear him. He reached out to grip the sides of the hole and slid his feet out. He dangled from his hands for a split second before dropping all the way to the ground. He caught himself on hands and knees and stood slowly, almost dramatically, and suddenly every eye in the room was focused on him.

He spared a brief glance at Nevada, who was smiling in relief, and another at Gramps, who was frowning in disapproval at the drama of the situation, before turning his sharp glare on Uncle Stephen.

"Actually," Taylor repeated, "I've been a bit busy trying to avoid the assassins you sent after me, Uncle. Did you really think you could hire assassins to come to Kensey, and we wouldn't notice? Especially after you snuck the hyenas in?"

"Preposterous!" Uncle Stephen tried to bluster, but Taylor's quiet scoff undermined his fury and returned all eyes to him.

"We followed the money trail you left when you hired the hyenas. We found the same trail attached to the assassins. Except, you want to know something funny, Uncle?" Taylor paused as if waiting for Uncle Stephen to respond, but wasn't surprised when his rhetorical question wasn't answered. "The funny thing is, the assassins weren't in the city yet when Antony was murdered. Uncle, when I follow the money trail again, will I find the car you hired to transport his body? Or were you stupid enough to use one of your own cars? I assure you, our DNA swabs will be quite thorough."

"This is ridiculous!" Uncle Stephen snapped. "Carley Lensington—"

"You're the one who approached me about Carley Lensington," Uncle Jeff suddenly cut in. He was standing tall, and the overwhelmed look was gone from his eyes. Maybe he would do all right as Carley's second, Taylor thought fleetingly before refocusing on the matter at hand. "You came to me with that evidence and demanded I arrest him immediately, except, now that I've gotten a chance to look through that evidence, I can see how superficial it all was. Testimony from a pair of drug addicts? And the surveillance tapes you had me look at were doctored. Made me wonder what you were really after."

"Power," Taylor said. "He wants to be sitting where Lord Kensey is right now. With me out of the picture and all evidence pointing toward Lord Kensey's incompetence being the cause, you planned to step in and take the crown for yourself."

"I never!" Uncle Stephen began but was cut off again.

"Don't lie to me, Stephen!" Gramps roared. He was standing now, but he hadn't moved forward, and suddenly Taylor understood why Gramps was so respected. Where Uncle Stephen and Uncle Jeff both looked the part, they lacked the sheer presence Gramps exuded. No one else in the room came close. "Admit your guilt, and you will only be punished for Antony's murder. Drag this out, and I will punish you for attempted regicide as well."

"You would allow that mongrel to be lord here, when you have so many humans you could have chosen instead?" Stephen snarled, pointing at Taylor with a shaking hand. "No. No, I won't allow it. I'll kill you all before I let that happen."

Uncle Stephen's hand dove into his jacket, and Taylor caught a glimpse of a laser gun, but Taylor was already moving, sprinting toward Stephen because Taylor knew the first shot would be for Gramps and the second for himself. He had to stop Stephen.

There were screams in the air, and the hot ozone smell of guns fired. Taylor was pretty certain he heard the scrape of ceiling tiles, and then the snarl of wolves entering the fray, but his eyes were focused on Stephen, who was already pointing his gun at the dais. Taylor ran right into him, letting his momentum throw them both to the ground. They hit with a jarring thud that made Taylor's ears ring, but there was no time to be dazed. He went for Stephen's gun, his claws digging into Stephen's wrist, trying to keep him from firing off any shots, to get him to drop the gun, anything to keep Gramps and Nevada safe.

Stephen's free fist jammed into Taylor's side, glancing off his ribs and into the tender part of his stomach. Taylor gasped at the flare of pain and had to drop one hand from the gun to block a second hit.

"You think your mongrel half is strong enough to stop me?" Uncle Stephen gasped out, and Taylor blocked a fist to the head with his forearm.

Taylor smiled widely right into Stephen's face, showing off his fangs even as his claws ripped a strip of skin off Stephen's thumb. But the bastard wouldn't drop the damned gun!

"I think my human side is more than strong enough," Taylor replied before quickly shifting sideways when Stephen tried to knee him in the stomach. "And my wolf side only makes me better."

"Mongrel," Stephen hissed.

"Traitor," Taylor hissed back.

Taylor blocked another fist, this time aimed for his throat, and snarled. Enough of this. The claws in his blocking hand swept down and across, cutting a deep slash over Stephen's chest and stomach. He slashed again, and this time Taylor stopped Stephen's fist point first. Blood flowed, slick and warm. The sour tinge of copper filled the air, and Taylor allowed himself to grin tauntingly at Stephen, his fangs back on display.

Stephen tried to knee him again, and Taylor responded with claws. More blood flowed, dripping onto the floor around them. And then, finally, Taylor heard a clattering sound as Stephen's gun hand convulsed in Taylor's grip. Taylor rolled off Stephen and felt the gun shift under his arm. He pinned his arm in place, using friction to slide the gun farther away, and when he rolled to his knees, Taylor was able to grab the gun and point it right at Uncle Stephen.

Taylor didn't think Stephen had noticed. The man was limp and bleeding, panting desperately for breath and shaking from pain. His entire chest and stomach were one giant laceration, and blood pooled in an ever-increasing circle around him.

"That's enough," Taylor said softly.

Uncle Stephen's head turned slowly to look at Taylor. "You think killing me will end it?" he gasped out, his voice choppy and his words starting to sound mangled like a drunk. "The Federals will finish this for me; just you wait and see." And then his eyes slid closed, and his body went slack.

Dead or unconscious, Taylor didn't care. What he cared about was stopping the chaos surrounding him before someone else got hurt. He stood, and this time his voice was a yell that echoed through the room, cutting through the screaming, the snarls, and the other sounds of battle.

"That's enough!"

Heads turned, and Taylor was gratified to see his wolves immediately stepped back from their prey. Other bodies lay on the ground. Mostly guards, although Taylor didn't know whether they had died as traitors or by fighting the traitorous guards while protecting the innocents in the room. Uncle Jeff's body had a smoking hole where his left lung used to be. Jeff had died protecting Gramps from the shot Stephen had fired before Taylor got to him, and Taylor was surprised at the twinge of sadness that tightened his throat. He hadn't really liked Uncle Jeff, but Jeff had been trying to become a better person. There wasn't time for that emotion now, not when there was no sign of Gramps or Nevada on the dais.

"Your leader is defeated; the coup has ended," Taylor continued into the quieting room. "Surrender!"

To his surprise, they did. Guards dropped their guns; one or two courtiers put their hands in the air. Taylor saw Larry, Stephen's youngest grandson, drop to his knees.

Taylor looked around the room, catching the eye of the guards who hadn't defected, and then turned to his wolves. "Secure the traitors and get the medical staff in here now." His gaze kept sweeping the room, hoping to find a flash of white fur. He saw black fur instead, and Shaw on his knees next to Craw, his hands clenched tightly over a deep gash in Craw's side and tears rolling down his cheeks. "Get me Oliver now!" Taylor added for effect, but he had already heard the squawk as someone spoke into their walkie-talkie.

Where was Nevada? Taylor kept looking and finally noticed the half-open door next to the dais. Of course, he thought with some relief. Nevada would have insisted on getting Gramps to safety, and Gramps would have wanted to get Nevada somewhere secure. Escaping out the side door made sense. Taylor strode forward, cutting through the crowd and hopping up onto the dais. He yanked the door open and let out a stuttering gasp.

Nevada was in the hallway on the other side of the door. He was standing a few feet away, his back to the door as he stood guard. A quick look didn't reveal anything amiss. His shoes were off, and the claws on his toes were bloody. Even the claws on his hands, shorter thanks to years of his filing them down, were tinged red. His tail was big and poofy, his ears pert, and as he finally looked over his shoulder to investigate the noise, his smile was a welcome ray of light in an otherwise terrible day.

"Hey, boss," Drew said from Nevada's left. Taylor turned to look and saw Drew's right arm was hanging. Dislocated, probably, or maybe a broken collarbone. Gramps was standing next to him, leaning against the hallway wall with a gun held loosely in one hand. Mike was below them. Shy, retiring Mike was sitting on Jerry's back, both of Jerry's arms twisted behind him so Mike could hold him down. Uncle Stephen's older grandson hadn't been able to stay out of the fighting after all, and Mike had his fangs out as fiercely as any of Taylor's wolves.

"It's done," Taylor said to them all. Gramps's firm, approving nod and Nevada's relieved smile were the last bit of validation Taylor needed to end this day. And then the medics descended on them and a different sort of chaos erupted.

Nevada, relieved from his position of making sure no one tried to ambush them from farther down the hall, joined Taylor. "Are you okay?" he asked softly.

Taylor reached out to run his fingers over one of Nevada's little ears, but stopped when he saw the blood all over his hands. Later. There would be plenty of time for that later.

"A little bruised, but none of the blood is mine," Taylor replied. "You?"

"Same."

Nevada let out a heavy sigh, and apparently not caring about the blood, he leaned against Taylor's side. His head rested against Taylor's shoulder, and all was right with the world. And that cute, fluffy little ear was right there. Taylor tasted the soft fur just a second before his teeth nipped, and then Nevada jumped away with a yowl.

Taylor knew his grin was full of carnal promise, of the knowledge of what a few little nips in the right place might lead to. Nevada rubbed irritably at his ear for a brief moment, but when he looked up, his own smile echoed Taylor's, except Taylor could also see the promise of revenge too. And that...that was perfect.

Epilogue

The pack house had never been so full. The entire pack was there, of course. Drew was holding court from his corner of the couch, regaling everyone yet again with the story of how he had broken his collarbone but managed to save Gramps's life in the process, and then Mike had finished the job while Nevada beat the crap out of a pair of guards. His arm was strapped to his chest to prevent him from moving it, and Hex was nursing him back to life by purring furiously in his lap.

Hex had competition though, which was something that made Taylor and Nevada giggle happily when they were in private. LeeAnne had been hovering protectively around Drew from the first moment he had been released from the hospital, and Drew was enjoying the hovering. Hex wasn't enjoying it, which was hilarious.

Shaw and Craw were sharing the large armchair placed adjacent to the couch. Craw was still pale and weak, his entire middle was wrapped heavily in bandages, and he was on even more serious painkillers than Drew, but Craw would also be okay after another month or so of bedrest and a lot of physical therapy. Shaw seemed to be taking good care of him.

Carley was standing next to the doorway into the kitchen, a glass of water in one hand. Despite missing the actual battle, he looked exhausted, which made sense. He had been working flat out on fixing the fallout from the coup from the second he had been released from house arrest. This was probably the first time he had stood still in weeks.

Even Gramps had stopped by, but he had already headed back to the manor, claiming he wanted to let the "kids" have their fun.

Drew's story ended, and there was a moment of pleasant silence. Nevada let out a sigh and slumped farther down on the couch. His head ended up on Taylor's chest, but his ears were too low to play with properly, which was probably Nevada's intention. That was okay. Taylor had plans later for those ears—and for the rest of Nevada too.

"Has there been any word about who was backing your uncle's plot?" Shaw asked. He had been speaking up a lot more lately, especially since Craw had been incapacitated for so long and he needed to be the voice for them both.

Carley stepped forward and finally settled into an open seat at one of the couches. "I've been hearing rumors about the Federals for years, but I never put much stock in their viability."

"What are they?" LeeAnne asked.

Carley snorted in disgust. "I don't know how much history of this country you know, but before the Great War that fractured the country into the city-states we have now, the country used to be run by one central government. Each city could create laws of its own, but they had to fall within the restrictions of that overarching government, which at the time was called the Federal Government. The Federals aren't that organized, but they are that ambitious. They want to take over all the city-states and combine them under their one banner, and it seems they found a way to attempt that here. We've managed to ferret out their entire operation in Kensey, so don't worry about them trying again anytime soon, and we've alerted all of our trading partners to be on the lookout too."

"So, this was all some plot to take over the city and add it to some collective?" Drew asked with a growl of disgust.

Carley nodded. "They've taken over a few smaller cities, but only the ones that were running rather peacefully. They wouldn't dare touch somewhere like Morse or Vegas, and I would have thought they would stay away from a city with an established and well-entrenched government like Kensey."

"Which means Uncle Stephen invited them." Taylor let out a sigh and curled his arm comfortably around Nevada. "They took advantage of his weakness, and six innocent people were killed plus ten guards and Uncle Jeff in the fighting." And Antony, but he had probably volunteered too.

"Either way, I'm not worried about them right now. Kensey is secure, and no one dares doubt your ability as heir, Taylor." Carley shrugged. "I'm more concerned about the jewelry thieves that have been hitting shops all over the city. Do you think your pack is up for some sniffing around?"

"Everyone except Drew," Taylor replied easily.

"Aww, man," Drew groaned.

"Only once your collarbone is healed," LeeAnne snapped. Hex mewled in firm agreement from Drew's lap.

Taylor didn't even need to add his own denial to the mix as Drew slumped unhappily in his seat. Instead he focused on getting his team ready.

"If we're going to be sniffing around all day tomorrow, we should probably get some sleep," he said to the room, almost all of whom promptly groaned.

Carley looked over at Shaw and Craw. "Can I give you a ride home?" he asked, rather redundantly, in Taylor's opinion, given he had driven them here, but Taylor saw Craw's appreciative smile. The city owed those two so much and touches like that were an easy way to say thanks, but Taylor knew Shaw and Craw were also growing on Carley. Shaw wasn't going to quit cooking anytime soon, but Craw might move to Carley's team in the near future.

They began the lengthy process of getting Craw upright, so Taylor nudged Nevada, who groaned, but obligingly got to his feet.

"We'll walk," Taylor said, watching Nevada yawn adorably.

He led the way to the door, then outside onto the street. Nevada's apartment wasn't far, but it was still a decent walk, except Taylor only walked a few feet down the street before he stopped and turned to look at the dark house next door to the pack house.

"This house is going on sale next week," Taylor said softly, and then shut his mouth on the rest of what he wanted to say. He couldn't look at Nevada, not when he desperately wanted Nevada to agree to move in with him. The location was ideal in that it was close to the pack house, the mansion, and to Café Spice, but Taylor wasn't going to pressure Nevada into something he wasn't ready for.

Nevada was rumbling with a purr when he pressed against Taylor's side, burrowing against him until Taylor's arm was forced upward to curl over Nevada's shoulders.

"Yes. When can we have a tour? Will you take down the fence between the two houses so the pack has more space to run? How much open space is there for my cats?"

Taylor laughed and hugged Nevada tight. "I'll call the realtor in the morning and set up the first available tour, and then we can knock down walls and do whatever renovations you want."

"Whatever renovations *we* want," Nevada corrected firmly.

Nevada was curled against Taylor's chest, so warm and so comfortable, Taylor wanted to hold him like this forever. Except, that ear was right there, so cute and fluffy. This was becoming an addiction, one Taylor had zero interest in resisting. He contemplated that ear for one last second, then arched his neck forward to take a nip. His mouth ran into the back of Nevada's hand, and when he looked down, Nevada was glaring up at him, both hands carefully covering his ears.

"No." Nevada slowly lowered his hands and then reached out to clasp one of Taylor's in his own. They started walking hand in hand down the street. "No more biting me in public," Nevada continued resolutely.

They continued walking for a few more minutes, Taylor enjoying sharing the quiet of the evening with Nevada, but he couldn't help pouting a little. Nevada must have sensed his disquiet. His grip on Taylor's hand tightened, and he started walking a little faster.

"It's just... You nip a lot in the bedroom too...and my body gets confused sometimes."

Taylor froze in place, yanking Nevada to a stop too. He used their shared hands to turn Nevada to face him and took in the bright-red tinge to Nevada's cheeks.

"Getting nipped turns you on?" Taylor couldn't help asking, although he kept his voice quiet, given they were on a public street.

"Yes," Nevada finally bit out. He yanked on their clasped hands, pulling Taylor back into a fast walk. "Now hurry up. You can't nip me here, but you can in my bedroom."

Taylor grinned and followed along happily, wondering if things could get any better. His city was safe, his family had survived, and his pack was growing. And, most importantly, he had Nevada.

Taylor knew the exact moment he had fallen in love with Nevada, and now he knew the exact moment when he had decided Nevada would be his forever. And he couldn't be happier.

About Mell Eight

When Mell Eight was in high school, she discovered dragons. Beautiful, wondrous creatures that took her on epic adventures both to faraway lands and on journeys of the heart. Mell wanted to create dragons of her own, so she put pen to paper. Mell Eight is now known for her own soaring dragons, as well as for other wonderful characters dancing across the pages of her books. While she mostly writes paranormal or fantasy stories, she has been seen exploring the real world once or twice.

Facebook

www.facebook.com/MellEightFiction

Twitter

@MellEight

Website

www.melleightfiction.weebly.com

Other NineStar books by this author

Oracle Series
The Oracle's Flame
The Oracle's Hatchling
The Oracle's Golem
The Oracle's Sprite

Supernatural Consultant Series
Dragon Consultant
Dragon Deception
Dragon Dilemma
Dragon Detective
Dragon Soldier
Dragon Adventures
Dragon Lesson

Out of Underhill Series
Kelpie Blue
If a Butterfly Don't Fly

Magnified Series
Magnified
Justified

Dragon's Hoard Series
Finding the Wolf

Breaking the Shackles

Stealing the Dragon

Melting the Ice Witch

Road to... Series
Road to Revenge

Road to Home

Wizard Wars Series
Ground of Insurrection

Ground of Resurrection

Standalone Books
Elemental Ride

A Little Fairy Dust

Wounded Alpha

The Coup and the Prince

Space Stars